The Cat Who Taught
Me How to Fly

The Cat Who Taught Me How to Fly

AN ARAB PRISON NOVEL

By Hashem Gharaibeh
Translated by Nesreen Akhtarkhavari

MICHIGAN STATE UNIVERSITY PRESS | EAST LANSING

♾ The paper used in this publication meets the minimum requirements
of ANSI/NISO Z39.48-1992 (R 1997) (Permanence of Paper).

Michigan State University Press
East Lansing, Michigan 48823-5245

Printed and bound in the United States of America.

26 25 24 23 22 21 20 19 18 17   1 2 3 4 5 6 7 8 9 10

LIBRARY OF CONGRESS CATALOGING-IN-PUBLICATION DATA
Names: Ghareayibah, Heashim author. | Akhtarkhavari, Nesreen translator.
Title: The cat who taught me how to fly : an Arab prison novel / by Hashem Gharaibeh ;
translated by Nesreen Akhtarkhavari.
Other titles: Qirtrt alladhei 'allamanei al-rtayarean.
English Description: East Lansing : Michigan State University Press, 2017.
| Series: Arabic literature and language series
Identifiers: LCCN 2016027172| ISBN 9781611862287 (pbk. : alk. paper)
| ISBN 9781609175139 (pdf) | ISBN 9781628952841 (epub) | ISBN 9781628962840 (kindle)
Subjects: LCSH: Prisoners—Jordan—Fiction. | Prisons—Jordan—Fiction.
Classification: LCC PJ7826.H297 Q5813 2017 | DDC 892.7/36—dc23 LC record
available at https://lccn.loc.gov/2016027172

Book design by Charlie Sharp, Sharp Des!gns, East Lansing, Michigan
Cover design and artwork by Shaun Allshouse, www.shaunallshouse.com

Michigan State University Press is a member of the Green Press Initiative and is
committed to developing and encouraging ecologically responsible publishing
practices. For more information about the Green Press Initiative and the use
of recycled paper in book publishing, please visit *www.greenpressinitiative.org.*

Visit Michigan State University Press at *www.msupress.org*

TRANSLATOR'S INTRODUCTION

The *Cat Who Taught Me How to Fly*, by Hashem Gharaibeh, is a unique prison novel where reality and fiction intertwine through a well-constructed narrative, breaking the traditional novel's structure and defying political, religious, and sexual taboos to boldly tell of human suffering, resilience, and the quest for the freedom to think and believe. Laced with Arab cultural images, practices, and perspectives presented through prison experience renders it exotic and familiar at the same time. It is not a biography, but the author's utilization of his decade as a prisoner in Jordan to create a literary work that mixes fiction with reality. The novel is an artistic rendition of a journey of a young Arab prisoner navigating through a new world, and his struggle to keep his dignity and hold fast to the right to differ, despite threats and incentives. The author takes us into prison life and intimately introduces us to the people that occupy that life. He is ever-present in the novel, as if to remind us that he was there. The journey is informative, thrilling, haunting, enjoyable, and bold.

ABOUT THE AUTHOR

Hashem Gharaibeh was born in 1953 in Hawara, a quiet agricultural town near Irbid, Jordan. His father was a successful farmer and well-respected tribesman. His mother, like many Jordanian women, was the glue that kept the family together and rooted in tradition, and was the source of strength and comfort to her children. Hashem spent a happy childhood in Hawara surrounded by his extended family, and then commuted to nearby Irbid for his high school education. He received his first bachelor's in dentistry labs from Baghdad, Iraq, in 1974 and another bachelor's in business and economics from Yarmouk University in Irbid, Jordan, in 1990. He is a member of the Jordanian Writers Society and served on its executive board for two terms, occupying the position of vice president from 1992 to 1994. He also served as Irbid Municipality's chief cultural officer, and as the chair of Irbid Festival as the City of Culture for 2007.

Hashem is a prolific, award-winning writer with over thirty published books and literary works. He is a member of the Socialist Thought Forum. He was imprisoned in Jordan for his political activism and membership in the Jordanian Communist Party for over eight years (1977–1985 and 1989). Many of his stories, plays, and novels reflect his prison experience. His stories include "Homoum Saghera" (Small Worries, 1980), "Gessas Oula" (First Stories, 1984), "Galb al-Madina" (Toppling of the City, 1992), "al-'Hayat Ebra Thoqoub al-Khazan" (Life through the Hole in the Water Tank, 1995), "Adwa al-Kalam" (The Contagiousness of Talking, 2000), and the collection *Habat Qamh* (A Grain of Wheat, 2014).

His novels include *Bayt al-Asrar* (The House of Secrets, 1982), *al-Maqama al-Ramlieh* (The Sand Maqama, 1998), *al-Shabandar* (The Shahbandar, 2003), *Petra Malhamat al-Arab al-Anbat* (Petra: The Epic of the Nabataean Arabs, 2007), *Petra—Awraq Ma 'bad al-Katab* (Petra: The Scrolls of the Temple of the Scribes, 2008), and *al-Qet al-Lathey 'Alamany al-Tayaran* (The Cat Who Taught Me How to Fly, 2010).

Gharaibeh also wrote children's stories, among them "Ghorab Abyad" (A White Crow, 1996) and "Ghozlan al-Nada" (The Deer of the Dew, 2000). He also wrote numerous plays and scripts for radio and television.

In addition to his essays and articles in national and regional newspapers, Gharaibeh served as the chief editor of *al-Mahata al-Thagafieh* (1995–1998) and *Baraeem Amman* (1998–2000). He received a number of awards, including the

Jordanian Writer Society's Mahmoud Saif a-Deen al-Irani's award for short stories in 1990, Arab Pioneer's Shield for his literary contribution from the Arab League in 2000, and Nazal Award from the Amman Municipality in 2008.[1]

Hashem's early years in Hawara, and its people and their simple life, shaped his thinking, fired his imagination, and heightened his sense of belonging. Describing that period, he wrote, "When I was a child, the sky was close to me. I would occupy myself counting its planets and stars, and drawing near to it until it engulfed me and became my friend. I would play with it, and almost catch its falling stars. Its clouds would circle around me like a flock of birds. The sky was near; its door was easy to open on the Night of Destiny.[2] Kind and evil people alike, just like me, were friends of its sun, which never discriminated."

His fascination with stories started at an early age as he listened to his mother's bedtime stories and his grandfather's tales, which shaped his language and ability to narrate with ease. In *Habat Qamh* (A Grain of Wheat), a collection of his short stories published in 2014, he wrote,

My grandfather was a skilled storyteller. . . . People liked him because he told stories in the evenings after long days of work. The people of the village used to gather around him and say, "Come on, tell us what you saw today."

He would start, "At dawn, I saw in the plains, a genie playing a reed with beautiful she-genies dancing around him. When I approached, they ran away like a swarm of elk!"

"Tell us more; what did you see?"

"When I arrived at the wheat field, I saw a virgin made of wheat, her hair a bundle of night that she combed with a golden scythe. When I approached, she flew away with a flock of grouse."

"Tell us more. What did you see?"

"Just before sunset, I saw an old man made out of silver perform his ablution in sunlight. . . . When I greeted him, he climbed the rays and disappeared behind the horizon."

People loved him because he told stories. He went out one morning, as he did each morning, and came back with a vision:

He saw the valley's beautiful genies, he saw the women made of wheat, and he saw the old man made from silver. People gathered in the evening and asked, "Come on. Tell us: what did you see today?"

He smiled calmly and said, "I saw nothing."[3]

Hashem's active involvement in politics at a charged time in the region, including the 1967 War, shaped his thinking and influenced his writings. His membership in the Communist Party in Iraq and then Jordan had him blacklisted in Jordan. After his return from Baghdad, he could not get a job, so he enrolled at Yarmouk University, taking a leadership position in student movements and party politics. He was arrested in 1977 and sentenced to ten years in prison, to be released in 1985 after serving seven and a half years. He opened a dentistry laboratory in 1985 with the help of his family, and has worked there since then. He was exiled to the city of Tafelieh in the south of Jordan in 1986 for his role in the Yarmouk University students' protests, and sent to prison again in 1989 following the "Bread Uprising" in Jordan, to be released after six months when Jordan lifted martial law and reinstituted parliamentary life and political parties. After his release, he went back to Yarmouk University and graduated in 1990 with a degree in business and economics.

The 1967 War, which Hashem witnessed, abruptly changed the quiet life in his region. Following the occupation of what was left of Palestine by Israeli forces, Palestinian refugees escaping the war flooded into Jordan, especially Irbid, a city in close proximity to the border with the West Bank. Hashem vividly describes that day:[4]

I was a young boy flying a paper airplane. The wind blew and raised a handful of sand that drifted quickly between the narrow dirt roads, gathered a few dry leaves, and then accelerated and rose forming an active storm. The boy rubbed his eyes and continued to fly his airplane.

The children's make-believe bus driven by Ali drifted to the right of the street, leaving enough space for the Iraqi troops coming from Baghdad to pass them. Ali was holding the cover of a rusty can, steering the imaginary bus with a rope made of pieces of cloth and used to outline the children gathering in a rectangular formation. The end of the rope was tied to Nada's waist marking the back of the bus. The crowd of children moved, and Hassan's body touched Nada standing beside him. A beam of joy flowed through him and gushed from his eyes, concealed behind the dark glasses fastened around his head by a string. From the rear of the bus, Nada nervously whistled, warning the armored vehicles about their presence. Iraqi aircrafts roared at low altitude, heading west! A young man ran, yelling, "The war, the war has started!" The children's bus formation broke up, and my paper airplane crashed into the *f*ields of lentils. Suddenly, I became a grown-up!

He further described the impact of the war on the people and his own daily life: "The bitterness of defeat was suffocating. The flow of refugees impacted our lives negatively. I was in ninth grade. My school became two schools, a morning shift and another one in the evening to accommodate refugees. The number of students in each class doubled. They distributed cans of sardines and biscuits to both refugee and local students, and canceled the classes that I liked most—art, P.E., library, and creative writing—to give enough time to offer an evening shift for the refugee children. Politics occupied all, including me." During this time, he wrote "Sardines in Place of Land," which he did not publish until 1990.[5]

That period greatly shaped Arabs' thinking and perceived alliances. They believed that the American support of Israel was instrumental in Israel's victory against the Arabs. Meanwhile, Russia accelerated its effort in spreading its ideology in the region, and was perceived as the friend of the Arabs. Hashem explained: "After the defeat of 1967, everyone became interested in the Americans and the Russians. The Americans to us appeared to be with Israel, and the Russians insisted that they were with us. I sided with the Russians, of course."

The people in his town tried to ignore the changes in the city and continue their lives. He described them saying, "Our wells are full of water, our barns are full of wheat, and the nearby village of Shoneh can supply us with all the hay we need, so to hell with the Americans and the Russians too."[6] They desperately wanted their lives to go back to the way they were.

Hashem's study in Iraq, and in particular at the capital, Bagdad—which was the regional center of politics and a vibrant literary and artistic hub at the time—greatly shaped his intellectual and political orientation. Its bustling life fascinated the young Jordanian student and intrigued him. "In Baghdad," he wrote, "I discovered poetry and poets, cinema, theatre, art, music, history, and the intensity of modernism. There, I learned about Marx and socialism. I discovered the worlds of Dostoyevsky, Chekhov, Pushkin, Todorova, Neruda, Aragon, Hemingway, Walt Whitman, John Steinbeck, and Conrad. To Baghdad, I owe my modernity!"[7]

There, like many other Arab students of his generation, he felt that he needed to be part of a movement and join a party. He explained, "I was supposed to become Baathist, supporting the regime in Iraq, but I became Communist. It seemed that I never was keen on supporting any Arab regime!" The dreams of his generation were liberating Palestine, establishing Arab unity, and promoting socialism; the Communist Party at the time advocated that too.

Despite the political and intellectual impact that Baghdad had on Hashem, he remained grounded in his own culture. He was like many Jordanians who studied in Arab capitals or socialist countries and were ideologically influenced at the time, who returned to Jordan looking for solutions to the local politics and social issues in their own culture and community. Their writings remain an accurate testimony of their sincerity and search for their own freedom, and the freedom and prosperity of their people.

Gharaibeh's many stories, plays, and novels treated the social, historical, political, and cultural issues deeply rooted in his local community and were informed by his commitment to social justice. As for many Jordanian writers, including Jordan's most celebrated poet and writer, Tayseer al-Sboul,[8] Jordan has always been Gharaibeh's inspiration. He explained, "My stories grow in the fertile mixture of scents, sounds, and images that were stored in my childhood memory. From the life I live, the protagonists emerge, and from the future, the stories borrow the imagined. The engaged drama comes from man's eternal yearning to have free will, and his fantasy to conquer time. The characters of my novels are not spirits adrift looking for salvation, not angels or demons, but humans with sins and beauty, victories and crises. Characters that succeed in recording their bewildered journey in this life, on my papers." In order to be able to write about his characters from within, Gharaibeh embodies them: "My heroes are me—interacting, reincarnated, or transformed into the bodies of ordinary people, marginalized and privileged; people that I knew or read about. My imagination employs them in my tales as they appear in the mirror of my mind, which is constantly crowded by inquiries." This intimate relationship between the author and his subjects makes it difficult for him to take himself totally out of his work. This is most clearly present in the prison novel, where he dedicates a chapter in the middle of the novel to talk about the author—himself.

Hashem also believed that there is a cultural vacuum in our world that can be filled through theatre! He saw theatre as a stage for depicting life, and that we constantly perform; even "our child-play is a form of performance, a reflection of our earliest theatrical expressions, and our desire to alter reality and shake its composure." He understood that theatre is also audience and script, and believed that the script should embody a real people and depict their lives; otherwise, it is pointless. He saw the world as a large stage with different worlds revolving around each other, a crowd of beings in constant theatrical dialogue, performing for an audience and for themselves.

Gharaibeh started performing at the university theatre in Baghdad and then formed with other Jordanian artists Amon Group 47, writing, producing, and directing a number of plays in Amman. He utilized these experiences in prison, where he wrote and directed plays that depicted the life and worries of the prisoners. To make these plays a success, he trained his fellow prisoners and turned the prison yard into an evening theatre. The project was a great success and an amazing experience for him, for the prisoners, and for the prison administrators.

Based on these experiences, he skillfully incorporated theatre in his novel as smart, highly appreciated, random, and staged performances by his eponymous Cat. Certain characters in his work mastered and used their theatrical talent to entertain, educate, criticize, reflect, and share their inner thoughts and feelings protected under the mask of performance.

After his release from prison, Gharaibeh continued his work in theatre. In collaboration with the Theatre School at Yarmouk University, he wrote plays and worked with students on directing and performing them. This included a play for children.

Hashem wrote for children with the same enthusiasm and social commitment with which he produced his other work. His interest in children's literature started with his own children. He told them the stories he had heard from his mother and grandfather, and when he had no more to tell, he made up his own stories from what he knew about his children's lives. When the children liked one of his stories, he wrote it down and published it. This experience made him realize that the children of today are "born in a different time, and in a world that differs from my world."[9] He started reviewing the content, illustrations, and form of the books he bought for them, then carried out two research projects about Arabic children's literature, which he published in a book titled *Writing for Children*. He was appointed editor of *Bara'em Amman*, a children's publication supported by the Amman Municipality, and then was invited by the Ministry of Culture to be the editor of its children's publication, *Wisam* magazine. Perhaps this interest and experience in children's literature is what made Hashem comfortable placing images from childhood into his work, including this prison novel.

Whether he was writing a novel, a short story, a play, or a children's book, Gharaibeh always orbited around his homeland. He knows it well; understands its complexity, pain, and joy; connects to its cities and villages; and recognizes its past and present and their relationship to him. From this all, he wove his tales and constructed his plays. He explained, "My homeland is my village, where in a nearby cave the She Ghoul lived; the shrine of al-Khader surrounded with holiness and mystery, lit by lanterns fueled with olive oil and fear, and shaded by a tree, heavy with secret wishes tied in ribbons hanging on its branches. My homeland was the source of endless stories. Now, it is a tired body of villages, cities, refugee camps, barren deserts, and a large head, the capital Amman, with its bridges, tunnels, high towers, and the latest technology offerings. I live in the rift between the weak body and the big head. Between my simple childhood and complex present, between tribal social structure and the yearning for a modern civilization, among the embers of Salafism hidden away in our old spiritual hearths and the latest in scientific and technological revolution. This is where I am tempted to perform; I drink my coffee and write."

THE NOVEL

Hashem Gharaibeh admits that his novel *The Cat Who Taught Me How to Fly* is his favorite work: "a novel that carries my vision about life, and my fingerprint as a novelist." It documents his perspective of what happened in a Jordanian prison at a certain period, as a participant and observer of much of the novel's content, but that does not make it a history text. He explained, "I am not a historian who documents how things exactly happened, but a novelist who is trying to rescue the hijacked memory of our people and their way of life." His work is "a novel and a biography at the same time, a recollection of intimate memories, rebellion against the limitation of time and place—the prison—and rekindling of the lantern of transparent sadness within my soul. It is a testimony to the strong force of life that shines in the darkest corners of prison; an inquiry about the limitation of space leading to the question of time, where time is like water, takes the shape of the space it occupies."[10]

The Jordanian writer Eiad Nassar described it as "a museum of prison narrative and literature . . . a condensed artistic representation of free will escalated by crises that its young protagonist faces in prison, to evolve into a deep awareness of the value of freedom and the right of man to believe and resist oppression."[11]

As Abdul-Haqq suggested, Gharaibeh's novel is different from much of Arabic prison writings, which are in many cases biographies presented as literary fiction. Gharaibeh, on the other hand, "succeeded in mixing the imaginary with the real, the objective with the personal, and mashing the two in complete harmony to create an artistic fiction, in which the real is undistinguishable from the imagined, especially to readers not familiar with Gharaibeh's personal experience."[12]

The movement that took place in the Arab world initiated by the beginning of Tunis's Jasmine Revolution in 2010 ignited old dreams and the hope for a positive change in the region. Many activists saw it as an extension of their old struggle for freedom and democracy. *The Cat Who Taught Me How to Fly* was born at that period. Gharaibeh dedicated it to the spirit of Mohammad Bouazizi[13] and free will, creating a link between his generation and the new revolutions.

The idea of the novel started when Hashem was asked to serve as a consultant on the project to convert Irbid Prison into a museum. After more than thirty years, he was back in the place where he spent the first year of his long prison sentence. He explained, "The place brought back images and events that were buried deep in my mind. It resurrected people that I had forgotten, and woke up feelings that time had scattered."[14] This coincided with the announcement in the newspaper of the death of Jordan's most infamous thief, one of Gharaibeh's prison mates affectionately known as "The Cat." That inspired the title of a column he was writing for the newspaper, and later became the title of the novel *The Cat Who Taught Me How to Fly*.[15] Gharaibeh explained, "I returned to old papers that I wrote then, which had turned yellow with time, and realized the magic of writing with the Cobia pen that resists fading. As soon as I started writing, they all returned, covered with the dust of their sins, victories, and time, stripped, unaltered, as they really were. They ran toward me! I do not know how, but they were there. . . . The Cat jumped out and sat cross-legged on the keyboard. I smiled and told him: angels and devils are two sides of one coin. Then Asaf appeared, followed by the rest of the prison inmates, one by one. The images of the heroes, comrades, and political leaders took a step back. Their characters did not excite or interest me. This is how the novel was born."[16]

The novel is about two hundred pages divided into twenty short chapters. The events take place in Irbid Prison starting in 1977 and extending for a year and a half.[17] The prison, to a large degree, symbolizes the larger world that Gharaibeh lived in, and its protagonist, Imad, represents Gharaibeh's own struggle inside and outside the prison walls. The rest of the characters are as much the focus of the story as is the main protagonist. The novel was not written to glorify the protagonist, who represents the author, or to praise the ideology he went to prison for. It is a human tale, including men's weakness, strength, and humanity.

Contrary to much of Arabic prison literature, where the author focuses on one protagonist, the hero—in most cases him- or herself—Gharaibeh chooses ordinary people from the many characters he met in prison, and employs them in creating a world that is very similar in its construction to the larger world outside prison. The main protagonist, Imad, is a participant and observer of this new life, which also reflects his new learning and expanding awareness of self, others, and the world around him. The only thing that remains constant is the protagonist's determination to stay free: free to say "no" even if this stubbornness costs him ten years in prison. This intimate negotiation between the protagonist and himself about the validity of this position is what weaves the events together despite the fragmentation of the structure of the novel. It soars with the reader beyond the localization of place, the cultural dimension of the characters, and the specificity of the events to a global focus where people, regardless of their ideological, political, social, or religious orientation, meet.

In addition to utilizing his own experience as a political prisoner and his struggle to come to terms with the prison's torture and humiliation, Gharaibeh details daily prison life, and introduces us to inmates with complex personalities and issues. He does not shy away from social taboos, including, politics, religion, sex, and homosexuality. He provides an insider, panoramic look at prison as a space, with its politics, corruption, power, class struggle, and privilege that resemble life in society itself.

What makes *The Cat Who Taught Me How to Fly* compelling is its realism and boldness. Like other Jordanian writers, Gharaibeh writes with honesty and transparency, sharing with the readers the protagonists' most intimate moments and private thoughts, exposing us to human frailty and nobility at the same time, and opening a window into the writer's own mind, heart, and soul. The novel in its spirit, language, and intensity resembles the work of the renowned Jordanian writer Tayseer al-Sboul in his novel *You as of Today* and two short stories.[18] Apparently, Abdul Razak al-Safi, the editor of *New Culture* magazine in Baghdad pointed this out to Hashem when he read his first work, "Small Worries," in 1973. Gharaibeh met al-Sboul one time in downtown Amman and they had dinner at Hashem Restaurant.[19] Hashem recalls that al-Sboul was "friendly, kind, humble, and encouraging." That was the last time he saw al-Sboul, who tragically committed suicide the same year.[20] I think it would be intriguing to have more in-depth analysis comparing the two authors' styles and treatments of subject and place, in order to better understand their creative experience and possible trends that bound Jordanian writers, in general.

After a shocking description of torture and interrogation at the beginning of the novel, Gharaibeh moves quickly to daily life in prison, describing the protagonist's initial registration and introduction to his new life and the prison's hierarchy and structure. He introduces us to the inmates, their names, titles, characters, and initial stories. The characters gradually evolve and reveal themselves through real-life experiences with honesty and depth, exposing their most guarded secrets and intimate dreams. He also provides us with an inside look at prison politics, corruption, power, class struggle, and privilege within the prison walls that resemble to a large extent life in society at large. Even though Gharaibeh's novel was rooted in his socialist ideology, it was far from ideological rhetoric. He freely expressed his dismay with some Party practices that negatively affected him, even in prison. Despite that, he remained true to his views on social justice and freedom, which were not in conflict with his personal dreams and tribal norms. He wrote, "My dreams were bigger than the ideology I adopted, and the needs of my soul were definitely larger than what my body could accomplish. From Marxism, I kept Hegel's dialectic, which is still the force that fuels the drama in my writings." This honesty did not sit well with many of his Comrades and Party leaders, who expected a more glorified and committed position from the protagonist. But just like al-Sboul, Gharaibeh was interested in presenting his characters and what they evolved to be, talking about what bothered him, remaining true to the narrative and not bound by ideology, and free to speak his own mind, not what was politically and socially expected.

Hashem's stubbornness and keen sense of justice, which are typical of Jordanians, is what makes the novel a true testimony to human resilience. The protagonist knows, like Hashem himself, that all he has to do to be released is to "publicly denounce the Communist Party and declare his loyalty to the King and his wise government." Just like Hashem, the protagonist spends the term of his sentence trying to convince himself to do that, but cannot bring himself to do it. The statement for him is more than "two lines on a piece of paper." Not signing is his weapon of resistance, his imagined victory, and the way in which he preserves what he has left of dignity and self-respect. Unintentionally, this causes admiration among his fellow prisoners and guards alike, and earns him the title "the Comrade." With that, he manages to lead a prison strike, empower the participants, and gain additional privileges for all prisoners. This move on his part escalates the already existing struggle between him and the new prison administrator over power, privilege, and control. What keeps him alive at that point is his dream of freedom, which in the end is tragically realized.

The novel is not traditional in its structure; it is rich with multiple registers of language and text. The narrative employs Modern Standard Arabic, and the dialogue is Jordanian with a northern dialect. It includes political reports, poems, letters, descriptions of political events, sexual encounters, and homosexual urges, much of which are illegal or immoral in an Arab context. He also incorporates references to other literary works, both Arabic[21] and Western,[22] all seamlessly integrated, providing a rich and intriguing narrative. The novel includes ample drama, violence, and sex, but all are relevant and brilliantly serve the plot of the story and enrich its content. Gharaibeh's treatment of social, political, religious, and sexual taboos is direct, and in some cases boldly and bravely pushes the social and religious norms and boundaries. By doing so, the novel realistically and skillfully depicts life in an Arab prison and mirrors much of the norms and practices of the people that live outside it.

Hashem Gharaibeh took a dark and miserable place, and constantly tried to find beauty in it as a space and in the people that occupied that space. Flying was the symbol of this freedom; finding a spot beyond the prison wall in the wide, beautiful sky that took him back to his childhood was his focus and constant search. The protagonist in the novel finds it figuratively, but Hashem found it in real life. He is back living in a beautiful home in Hawara, with his wife and three boys, farming his land, managing his business, and writing, unrestrained, flying where his imagination takes him. Hashem admits that he wrote the novel thirty years after the prison experience because he needed to come to terms with the experience before he wrote about it, which he managed to do. His only regret is that with his stubbornness, he caused both his parents pain and suffering, which he better understood when he had his own children. He believes that he "had the right to say no, and pay for his position," but often wonders if he "had the right to make [his] parents suffer because of his stubbornness." That still causes him pain, and he hopes that the novel is "an accepted public apology to his parents."

TRANSLATING THE NOVEL

After reading this novel, I knew I wanted to translate it. It was about man's quest to be free. A lesson in human resilience and triumph, so relevant to what is happening in our world today. I wanted Western readers to know people like Hashem Gharaibeh, who was willing to give up his freedom to be truly free. I hoped that by reading it, people would discover the shared humanity in our experiences beyond the walls of color, gender, race, or political orientation. I kept thinking of the thousands of people in our prisons, and what they would discover out about themselves when they read it. I thought about my students and my friends, and their reactions.

I was a student at the University of Jordan when Hashem was serving his sentence at Irbid Prison. I know Hashem's hometown, Hawara, and the city of Irbid, where the novel takes place, is where I was born and spent my early childhood. The dialect that he used in the dialogue is familiar to me and brought back memories of places we have known in common. This made reading the novel easy and intense, and made translating it personal and profound. I met with Hashem many times during the translation process, which allowed me to ask questions about the novel and his experience. Talking to him also allowed me to gauge his feelings and reactions to the aftermath of the prison experience and writing it down to be publicly shared, with all its private moments. I found him at peace with it and with himself. This made it possible for me to go through the heartbreaking and awkward moments when I felt that the text was too private or too painful for me to tackle.

I was careful to remain true to the novel's text and to keep my feelings and reactions to myself. I want you to hear his voice, to feel his experience, and to understand it as he lived it.

DREAMS, MY NOVEL, AND ME: THE NOVEL *THE CAT WHO TAUGHT ME HOW TO FLY*

Hashem Gharaibeh, translated by Nesreen Akhtarkhavari

THE PRISONER

In prison, I never for a moment stopped thinking about running away. I constantly dreamed about flying. I could not stop thinking that the authors of those two books that helped me make it through the long prison years were pilots![1]

By learning—learning how to fly—what we try to do is soar beyond emptiness and the absence of meaning in our lives. We learn how to scale walls, climb the high fences imposed on us, and escape to freedom in life inside prison and in life outside it.

This is what helped me survive in prison: I learned to daydream!

When I closed my eyes, the isolation disappeared. I plunged into the vibrant depths of the universe. I felt I was beyond all obligation and stronger than any coercion. I became free without weight or pretense.

In solitary confinement, I did not even need to close my eyes for my memory to conjure images of a hot rock on a mountainside, of women washing their raw wool at the edge of a water hole, of flocks of migrating storks circling the horizon, or herds of goats waving their tails with joy. I could bring back fresh air wrapped in sunlight carrying the scent of jasmine and citrus blossoms, which would trigger memories of crows cawing or flocks of cooing doves singing praises to their provider.

During the long nights, I recalled the stars my parents warned me not to count for fear of warts growing on my skin. I would count them until they engulfed me and became my companions. I would imagine befriending them, playing with them, almost catching them, and watching them surrounding me like flocks of doves.

Sadness comes on its own. But moments of happiness need to be sought out and harvested.

We do not choose our experiences in life; experiences choose us. Nothing is more pleasurable than daydreams: the scent of my mother, jasmine, bread, olive oil, mint, and thyme. Daydreams: the sound of the morning call to prayer, birds chirping, water gushing along the gutter, my grandfather's strong voice singing sad old songs, light brown wheat stalks and large fields of poppies painting the face of the land bright red.

THE PRISON

The essence of the battle is this: how do we protect our privacy and ourselves from being violated and objectified? In prison, you can defy authority, you can manipulate space, but you can never escape time. Time is you.

In prison, a person has one of two choices regarding the senseless quick and slow passing of time. One path passes in a constant scene that is dull and monotonous, void of joy or amazement. It turns the prisoner into a whiner, constantly complaining about the smallest things, such as the cold of winter or the heat of summer. Meanwhile, life passes by like the pages of a calendar.

The other choice is to learn to fly free throughout a magical and ever-changing universe, to continually walk into each new day as you desire to live, feeling fortunate to be gifted with the capacity to intensely feel each moment. To live a life in which you take your first breath each morning with an enormous appetite and feel life pass like the gentle drop of jasmine petals onto the palm of your mother's hand.

In prison, I experienced the worst kind of living. But life itself was always bright and beautiful and worth fighting for. It was worth clinging to, worth slowly absorbing its intoxicating elixir.

In prison, I learned to daydream. I learned how to wait and how to think, how to be patient, and how not to regret what had happened in the past.

In 1982, the middle of my seven-year prison sentence, the market was strong and many managed to quickly become rich. As a result, we had to live with greedy residents whose prison sentences related to "tomato deals," "income taxes," "drinking-water," and "land and surveillance corruption." One of the wealthy men who joined us at that time liked to smoke his shisha as he walked. He would walk around the prison courtyard, followed by a servant carrying his shisha. He would slowly inhale the bay leaf–scented smoke, and then exhale it with an ego befitting a great conqueror!

That year also saw the greatest tragedy I ever experienced (through the radio)—at least I thought it was at the time—the tragedy of the occupation of Lebanon and the massacres at Sabra and Shatila. I still remember the voice of the Israeli announcer, Shaoul Manishieh, choking with pride as he described in a live broadcast the Israeli tanks landing at Junieh and then entering Beirut. During that period, I had written a play I called *The Vision*, and had written and directed other plays, including *The Enchanted Door, Standing on One Foot, Travel the World and Get Back Here*, and *The Stranger in the House*.

After Beirut's defeat and the bright economic boom that followed, we were allowed to remove some of the old walls that separated the cells from the prison courtyard. We found many things hidden in the walls—a publication of the Jordanian Communist Party written in the 1950s, decaying papers that belonged to the Baath Party stuffed between the cement bricks, and secret correspondence between political prisoners of various orientations. We also found a photo of Abdel Nasser, some official letters, political news from a past era, complaints, and love letters.

What an archive of pain it was! What a pleasure and privilege it was to read documents from a bygone decade of icons from Jordan's national resistance movement: Taqi al-Deen al-Nabhani, Muhammad al-Rousan, Abdallah al-Remawi, Eissa Madanat, Munief al-Razaz, Yaqoub Zayaden, and Ishaq al-Khateeb.

One night, the prisoners went to bed early in anticipation of an early rise the next morning in order to witness the hanging of a fellow prisoner. I stayed up reading al-Jaberty's daily scrutiny of Napoleon entering the Azhar Mosque, which coincided with the birth of a two-headed goat in Bawaq Alley. Then, a fight broke out between the Moroccans and the copper makers in the next cell. All this while occupied with the thought that a man would be hanged in the morning!

I thought about the innocent face of Imad Melhem, my Druze friend, who explained reincarnation to me and told me about a little girl who remembered her past life. His eyes glowed when he spoke about the Holy Trinity (the mind, the body, and the spirit) and the *Book of Wisdom* that was safely hidden in the trunk of a large tree in Khalawat al-Bayada in north Lebanon. Meanwhile, at my right was Ali al-Toueisy, who told me stories of the Arabs of the Bdool tribe[2]—the descendants of King Harith al-Nabataea[3]—and their strange ways, customs, and beliefs, and oral traditions about the wonders of the city of Petra, of Baida,[4] and the holiness of the trembling torrent.[5]

What fantasies occupied me during those long nights of prison! How could I ever put them on paper?!

A CULTURE

In prison, we were eager to read revolutionary books. Only historical and classical books were made available to reform us. In the mind of a young secular Communist, yearning for knowledge, the giants held debates with one another—al-Ghazali and Ibn-Rushid, Wasel bin 'Atta and Ahmad ibn Hanbal, Jamal al-Deen al-Afghani and Muhammad bin Abdul-Wahab, Muhammad Abdu and Hassan al-Bana, Abu al-'Ala' al-Mawdoudi and the Naferi, Ibn 'Arabi and Ibn Tamima, Jalal al-Din al-Rumi and Sayed Qutob, the biography of Ibn Hashem and the tales of King Saiph ben Dhi-Yazan, the Shahnameh, and Taghreibat Bani Hilal—a unique opportunity, an involuntary course of study, with time sufficient to cover that and more.

In 1982, when the morning star glowed over the Druze seclusion area of Khalwat al-Bayada,[6] its secret was exposed by the rumbling tanks of the god of war, dispersing the council of wise elders that surrounded the tree. At that time, I was searching for a way to write prison narrative different from anything I had seen out there. I wanted it to be far from complaining and whining, closer to an overflowing stream of life that would flood even the darkest corners of the prison.

The true test of a novel's protagonist is not his political affiliation, but his rebellious spirit, the scent of jasmine in his memory, the longing that burns in his heart, and the dreams that hover over that wide space, the universe. He found the echo of his dreams in two books that had nothing to do with politics or ideologies—*The Little Prince* and *Jonathan Livingston Seagull*.[7] In real life, the young prisoner found his solace in the friendship and support of a thief called "The Cat." The Cat was not the only friend he made. People in prison had welcoming hearts; their souls were wide open and accessible, but they were still the children of life with its prejudices and complexities.

The fledgling friendship between the young political prisoner and the thief with broad life experiences illuminates the other characters in the novel. From this, the novel expands and introduces us to a world different from the one we are familiar with, but at the same time, closely tied to what we know!

MIXED MEANING

This novel is a walk down memory lane, a journey that stretches across time and place and brightens the soft lantern of sadness in the soul. It is an account of the forceful flow of life pulsing at the darkest corners of prison. It is an exploration in the restriction of space, which opens into the question of time. Here, time is like water: it takes the shape of the place and, like other things, cannot be seen in darkness. The oil in the lantern of time is movement, and its wick, achievements. Even heaven is unbearable without achievements.

Now, when cities, streets, food, restaurants, haircuts, fashion, and love poems all start looking alike; when newspapers all turn into one paper (why don't they give the publishers stamps and slogans and let them make copies?); when fluff fills people's lives—media, sermons, lectures, conferences, and presentations—what happens to human beings? Then, depth and creativity require that people learn to fly!

BIRTH

In conversations with my friends, I do not talk about or refer to my experience, except when asked. I used to be repulsed by heroes bragging about their deeds, regardless of whether they were Comrades or writers. I used to feel the heavy weight of their inflated pride. When I was asked by friends and the media, "Why don't you write about your experiences in prison?" I would reply that it was not yet time for it.

I used to feel within me a sense of anger, of bitterness, and of pride—but it was a wall that stood between me and writing. I was leery of cheap talk about my experience, worried that I would be bound by it. I lived it and endured it as a free common man—free and common. It is said that freedom is the awareness of necessity. The law of necessity may force you to bend, but it does not force you to sell your soul, even to the most beautiful angels. I needed the right time and place to be free of myself and to be able to write!

On a rainy day at the end of 2012, the newspapers reported the death of the famous national thief, Said Muhammad al-Nabilsi, known as "The Cat." He was found dead at the Roman historical site of Sabil al-Horiat, the Path of the Handmaidens, in downtown Amman.

The news shocked me and triggered a stream of memories. I sometimes saw him in downtown Amman. He avoided me, and while other former prisoners avoided him, I never did. I thought of him, and the phrase "the Cat who taught me how to fly has died" flashed into my head.

I was happy with the phrase as a title for my weekly column—at the time, I was writing a column for the Jordanian *Al Ra'i* newspaper. I suddenly remembered I had written something about him when I was in prison. I took out the old leather bag that held what survived of my papers and drawings from my prison time and looked through it. At midnight on a rainy day, I woke up my family, screaming, "I've found it! I've found the notebook!"

It read:

When I was young and innocent, I had a kind mother who cared for me and saw the light of the world through my eyes.

I used to love words and songs.

My mornings were at school, my middays at public libraries, and my evenings with books spread out at the street corner. I used to return to my mother with bright words like painted clay.

My mother was a maid who collected leftover bread and scraps of clothes from the homes of wealthy people she worked for.

Meanwhile, I was occupied with nothing but that hopeless nonsense!

My mother fell ill, became an invalid, and died.

Did she die of hunger? No!

My mother did not die of hunger! She lived hungry. As a result, she got sick in the morning, her health failed her by noon, and she died before nightfall. She left me with nothing but a shack and a mulberry tree.

Believe me, Comrade, hunger can turn one into a beggar or a thief, but hunger does not make a rebel.

I chose to be the latter. Stealing is more honorable than begging. Ha! My interpretation!

The old yellowed page made me forget my weekly column, and I became occupied with writing a novel, *The Cat Who Taught Me How to Fly*.

I, as an author, found the contrast between the thoughts of the experienced writer, his rationale for the events that took place at the end of the 1970s, and his earlier views and perceptions, long decades ago, to be important, beautiful, and fascinating. Being a little distant from those events allowed me to see "the elephant in the abdomen of the snake" and "the sheep inside the box."[8]

I started the novel with an opening statement:

I, the novelist, Hashem Gharaibeh, was turning the pages of an old yellowing notebook I had written thirty-three years ago when a jasmine blossom the color of hay flew out like a butterfly. It landed on the palm of my hand and reached into my soul by a thin trace of jasmine scent mixed with the pride of youth, the age of inspiration, the warmth of a dream, and the sanctity of personal dignity. The writings of the indelible pen glowed, waking the memories sleeping in the palm of time.

This was included in the middle of the novel.

SHOULD I CONFESS?

The novel relates the story of one year, the period during the novel, sifted from my seven years' experiences behind the high windows, thick walls, and barbed wire of prison. It stretches in time and place to cover a young man's life and the history of a wide space, but it is still centered around a prison building. Irbid Prison is where the events of the novel take place, but the story includes memories from other prisons I lived in, including:

- The National Intelligence Prison, a number of cells on the lower floor of the National Intelligence Building, beneath the interrogation offices and the torture chamber.
- Irbid Prison, which I describe in the novel.
- Al-Mahata Central Prison and the unforgettable memories of Cell 14, where two of us Communist prisoners were incarcerated. The section held thirty-seven political prisoners, housed in sixteen cells.
- Al-Jafar, a desert prison of three domed military buildings, each

approximately fourteen meters long. It was a remnant of an old English military barracks, used only to house political prisoners with long sentences.

- Al-Tafieleh Prison, a small jail inside the police headquarters of an isolated town. It consisted of three cells and a courtyard. Most of its occupants were from the town; the prison usually did not exceed two to fifteen prisoners. I was moved there after my attempt to escape from Irbid Prison.
- Swaqa Prison, a huge modern prison built to American penitentiary standards. It sits at the edge of the desert highway, south of the capital.

I confess. The characters in the novel are thieves, crooks, embezzlers, killers, drug dealers, guards, shoplifters, bullies, officers, informants, and interrogators. They are the other face of the politicians that I encountered. I was always thinking of people I knew and imagining them as party leaders, rebels, and activists! I would observe their faces while they slept, while they engaged in discussions, while they walked in the courtyard and ate their food. I would notice they were like the rest of the convicted occupants of the prison, and I wondered what gave us the right to classify ourselves as good and the rest as evil. There, in the prison, I saw the angels and the devils as two faces of one coin.

"Prison tests us without appeasing and strips us without limits."

I gave them new features, different from the ones they had, from what was on their prison records. I portrayed them during breaks—squatting in venerable positions, eating at variable degrees of dignity, and showing off their pride when meeting their visitors. I drew them from the inside, from behind their ideological masks. That is why I did not choose a major prison as the setting of the novel. I chose one that I knew well, had had experiences in, and one that did not have a strong presence of political prisoners. When developing the novel's characters, I also recalled the personalities of political figures I had known and had lived with for over two-thirds of my sentence. I was right in my assumptions about them!

I love my activist Comrades and friends, but they want me to show them as heroes—proud, glorious, and resisting. Instead, I wrote about what happened inside me, about my own hesitation, weakness, desires, and worries. For that, the novel did not meet with the approval of my freedom-fighter Comrades. They did not like what I said about myself. What would they have done if I had written those things about them? They want the image of a glorious, exemplary, resisting hero, but with no meat!

The body is caring and forgiving. It always forgives the faults of the mind and accepts and adjusts to sickness, deprivation, and prison. Still, we judge it and label it as inferior to the mind. We are ashamed of revealing its concerns! That is why when the body drops out of the game, it drops in an instant, and forever, leaving us hanging in a void.

People love heroes. They need strong icons. I am neither a hero nor a true idol. I am a common man who sees people—including heroes and saints—as a mix of angel and devil at the same time. My time there was seven and a half years full of waiting, patience, learning, and living with all types of people.

The novel compresses those seven prison years into one. Seven different, dark, gloomy prisons, all with different buildings, different ways of living, different inmates, and different types of prisons, all placed into Irbid Prison.

IN GENERAL

The Tree of the Knowledge of Good and Evil was chopped down before it reached maturity. The flood came to absolve people of their sins, and became the tale. Then the people became full of pride again and built a tower of vanity in Babylon. Their tower collapsed and everyone was anxious to tell the story! The tales multiplied and the people started fighting and killing for tales that they had turned into certitude.

In general, there is a fine, thin, jagged, deceptive, and changing line that separates opposites. They seem distant, divided, and in contradiction with one another. But they are at the same time close, intertwined, and separated only by this fine, deceptive line. Like great deeds and lowly actions, the real and the imaginary, good and evil, freedom and injustice, the ideal and the wretched, the model and the statue, intertwine.

Art, with its bright wings, touches differing and contradictory subjects and illuminates the thin line that separates the wheat from the weeds, night from day, life from death, and freedom from prison. It illuminates what was hidden from the eyes of the passersby, separating what appeared connected, and joining what seemed separate.

No matter how much light I shed on the process of my novel's birth, an author's choice of his subject remains a mysterious ritual. The mountains cannot comprehend how the spring settled inside them, drop by drop, until they erupted and spilled over, forming rivers and lakes.

We do not know how all our small sorrows gather in the soul, or how small joys excite us to break into life. We do not know how ideas combine and how images deposited in our unconscious become a narrative worth living, or how our narrative becomes our novel about life.

I wrote my novel without logical analysis and thoughtful theorizing. I wrote it outside the logic of official history and beyond the influences of Internet, television, and the pulse of rapid communication. Meanwhile, Gilgamesh continues to comfort my wounds with his great tale, propelling me to dream about immortality and seek possession of supernatural powers to triumph over time—distance!

I still dream of flying.

The Cat Who Taught
Me How to Fly

The Stranger's Cage

In the morning, Imad watched the prisoners gather by the wire fence inside the prison, and saw them looking at the new prisoners being transferred from the National Intelligence Detention Center. It reminded him of the circus that pitched its tent in Irbid municipality's playground a few years earlier—a scene that inspired his colorful paintings and won him his teachers' admiration.

The bus to his village only ran during the day. The circus, on the other hand, opened at night! His cousin Asaf caught a donkey roaming in the field and announced with a lisp that became more pronounced when he was excited, "Come, let's ride the donkey and go to the circus."

They both rode the donkey and went to watch the circus. He remembered watching the show with Asaf that evening, but could not think of the details of how Asaf managed to trade the donkey as feed for the tigers in exchange for admission into the circus. After the show, they had gone home on foot.

He also remembered the day they went with their friends to Irbid to watch the Indian movie *Sinjam*. They ended up shedding tears for five hours! They went back home that night riding donkeys and singing, "Mary manki gumna, mary menki jumna, bour rasa, bour sanja, bogaki nahi."[1]

"Hello cousin! Thank God for your safety." He recognized Asaf's face among the crowds watching them from behind the screen and answered back, waving his hands, "Mary munki jumna . . ."

■　　■　　■

After middle school, Imad went to high school in Irbid. Every morning, he had to pass by the front entrance of the old gray prison, climbing the hill to get to his new school. He would imagine wild creatures behind bars, roaring with rage, trying to break out of their cages, or crouching in a corner pretending to surrender while thinking of a way to escape!

Now that he had entered the cage, he recalled Zakari Thamer's play *The Tigers on the Tenth Day*. He wondered bitterly, "Am I on my first day? Why did I put up with three treacherous months of torture and agony at the Intelligence Detention Center?"

He swallowed the bitterness of his question, lingered at the space in the courtyard where shadow and sunlight met, then turned back and walked into the warmth of the sun. He hoped that getting to prison would be a break from the endless torture, the suspension, flogging, and constant bright lights at the Detention Center.[2]

With time, he learned to control his senses and was able to put up with the different methods of torture used on him during interrogation. After each round, they threw him back into his cell, bleeding and happy! He managed to resist giving up, confessing, or providing them with the information they wanted. He was winning! That feeling of triumph made him more able to endure the agonizing hours of suspension that followed. They would tie his hands to the dark blue metal bars above the window on top of the door of his cell and leave him hanging for hours. Time would pass and turn his mind into a gray zone, where it was hard to distinguish if it was a slice of a day or part of the night. His daydreams helped him pass time; he would imagine himself on another planet playing with the Little Prince, dredging the scent of jasmine out of his memory, and thinking of the pleasure of defying them with his daring silence. With anticipation, he patiently waited for the incredible moment of happiness when they would untie his hands!

Beating was easier than suspension. Maybe because after the beating sessions, he could clearly see the disappointment on the faces of his interrogators, while suspension placed him in front of the silent wall of time—a slow, constant, painful torture that lasted until his hands were finally untied, usually by a guard who showed no vengeance and dared not sympathize.

This time was different from all other times of torture that he had faced with stubbornness and steadfastness. They used a new method that had never crossed his mind. He was warned by the literature from the Party and the tales of ex-prisoner Comrades who told about their travails, but he had never heard of this one. They took him to the torture chamber, chained his hands behind his back, and then tied his big toe to the tip of his penis with a short nylon thread! They stood watching him! He tried but could not recall the tale of *The Little Prince*, and he was unable to bring back the scent of jasmine. His body was beat in minutes, and he became consumed by an unbearable pain that stretched from his spinal cord and rose up to his head like a ball of fire! He tried to recall the daydreams that he had mastered during the hour of suspension, but he could not.

In a moment of extreme cruelty, he felt as if the teeth of the gears of his brain were disengaging and turning aimlessly, displaying images and ideas out of control! He was very frightened, and the flag of surrender appeared to cloud his mind. The minute he decided to give himself up,[3] he fell unconscious.

When he woke up, he checked his penis and found it swollen; he touched it, and it moved. When he realized that it was still there, he felt better, and went back to a deep sleep with no dreams. After that incident, the torture stopped! But does it ever stop?!

He found himself alone, facing time with its weight, stillness, and stubbornness through the darkness of a lamp shining its bright light at him around the clock.

Loneliness is a barrenness that creeps into the core of the soul. In solitude, the bird of the soul flies from between the shoulders for forty autumns, yearns to find his home, gets old, and never reaches its destination.[4] He wished for a beating session that would offer him human contact and bring the memory of jasmine back to his senses.

A night in solitude is like a thousand nights.[5] How hard it is to face time without people. The river of time cannot be seen in the bright darkness, and its shores are not recognized by the strict repetition of meals or the time of bathroom breaks!

After what seemed like an endless time in isolation, they brought him a cellmate, a member of the Islamic Liberation Front, to keep him company. The jasmine bush flourished again, and the cell became twice its size by the presence of a partner to whom he could tell his favorite story, the story of *The Little Prince*. By having a cellmate, the place flourished; it became a debate hall, a chessboard, a train, and a golf course, too. A place for gambling on the number of ants in the cell, what breakfast would be the next day, and what the guard on duty would look like when they saw him next time.

They started treating him well, to the point that he started wondering if they might be releasing him.

One evening, the officer on duty came around doing checkups.

He said to the Liberationist, "Advise your friend, he is a stubborn Communist. He wants us to become like Russia. People there dream of a pair of jeans and cannot get any. Women prostitute themselves for a piece of gum. They have no hamburgers. Ha, ha, ha, and in Communist China, they don't even know what bread is!"

The Liberationist answered with an ill-timed response, "Take the jeans, and the gum, and the hamburger, and even the bread, and give us a great nation—a nation with self-determination."

"Wonderful! You are ganging up against us. Separate them!" ordered the officer.

They separated them, and the young prisoner went back to dipping his finger in tomato sauce and drawing on the wall a snake swallowing an elephant, which looked like a big squashed hat!

One morning, they allowed him to bathe, dressed him in civilian clothes, and allowed him to meet his father.

■　■　■

In the prison courtyard, his mind was crowded with questions that were on the tip of his tongue. For some reason, he did not ask them. His cousin Asaf met him cheerfully and carried his bedding—both as a friendly gesture and as family ties dictated.

In the Intelligence Detention Center, he had slept on a sponge mattress that was comfortable in comparison to this mat made of shredded old blankets sewn together with thick cotton yarn and saturated with the smell of DDT powder.

Asaf was two years older than he was. Two years seemed like a big difference for someone in his early twenties. This kinship traditionally obliged Asaf to take care of his younger cousin. They passed a water basin figuratively called a "pool" and walked by a group of men in suits, ties, and shiny shoes, walking briskly back and forth with seemingly no particular preference between sunny and shaded areas!

Asaf commented, "The masters of the White House."

The young man was surprised that there were masters and that they lived in a White House!

A woman made a cheerful yodeling from somewhere.[6] Asaf laughed, "Someone was released." He pointed to the southeast side of the prison and said carelessly, "Women's Section."

The young man continued to be amazed, and the scene was becoming more unfamiliar to him. He saw a group of children with scarred faces and tattooed arms diving in the "pool," splashing each other and making loud noises. Asaf scolded them, lisping, "Stop it! Don't splash!"

He wondered why the prisoners walked fast. Where were they going? He did not ask. He had learned to live with unanswered questions.

Asaf entered a long hall divided by two wide doors. He turned left and headed to the North Ward.[7] The new inmate followed him; he felt as if he was entering a large dungeon. The place was dark and full of old rotten stench, mixed with the smell of concentrated ammonia and fried onions!

The section had no distinguishing features except a large iron door; the floor was completely covered with inmates. He saw a line of termites climbing a rotten wooden window frame half the size of regular windows. From the frame, a spider dangled, weaving its web with care and patience.

Asaf had been in and out of prison from a young age. He started his career selling individual cigarettes to the students in school. This escalated when he sold a keg of olive oil to a merchant in Amman. The man soon discovered that it was a keg of water with a thin layer of oil floating on top. The crooked stole the money of the greedy!

Asaf's ability to scam and swindle was endless, but his experience as a prisoner was of tremendous help to the young inmate settling into this strange place.

Asaf made space next to him for his inexperienced cousin, with little objection from the other inmates, who were all engaged in conversation in the northeast corner, close to the small space where he placed his mat.

It was a terrible crowdedness, as each space was occupied; there was no place for anything on the floor or the walls. Every little space was used in one way or another.

Small, bare, protruding stones held up the ceiling. From them dropped lines of stripped electrical wire, bundles, plastic buckets, clothes, and scorched cooking pots, pans, and utensils by their ends.

On the western wall was a high black hole called a window, and to the east, two openings were used to store the prisoners' belongings. Between them, on the dark wall, was misspelled graffiti, written with a nail or sharp object: "created for pain," "all is the fault of women," "prison is for men" . . . (He would later see these phrases tattooed with a dagger, bow, arrow, or snake on the shoulders, arms, or chests of prisoners.)

An old man with a large nose asked him, "Anybody left out there?"

The young inmate answered, surprised, "Where there? What do you mean?"

"In Irbid."

"People?"

"People."

"Of course. Many."

"Will they be there for a long time?"

"What long time?"

"Ha, ha, ha . . ."

Everyone laughed.

The man sitting between the three of them asked, "Is the brother a thief or a robber?"

Asaf replied, lisping, "Your father is a thief and a robber!"

Another man turned to the young inmate and said, "I am Abu Haddid, the Leader of this ward. Of course, I need to know everything. What is your crime?"

Asaf replied, "Political."

"What political?"

The young inmate felt that "political" was too much for him, but he said nothing to the leader. The third old man remained silent, looking at the floor. His face seemed familiar to the young inmate. The leader continued questioning. "Is the brother PLO?"[8]

Asaf replied, "A Party member."

The questioning stopped when a guard with a small head, wide hips, and skinny legs came in waddling like a duck, a paper in his hand, and calling, "Imad al-Hawari."

The young inmate stood up. "Yes."

"Come, the Warden wants you." Imad left with the guard. "Hurry, and keep your hands behind your back." They passed the hall and waited between two large gates.

They were bringing in a new prisoner.

"Hello, Hayder."

"Hi, Younis." The guard returned the greeting.

"Give me a cigarette."

"Lulu?"

"I don't care. It can be *heishi*.[9] I've got to have one."

"A thief?"

"No, a killer. And yours?"

"A Communist."

"God forbid!"

Younis turned his face to the side, stretched his collar out, and pretended to spit three times inside it.[10]

A third guard, with yellowed skin, winked and pointed to an inside staircase leading to the upper offices. Hayder took Imad to the Warden.

His trip to the Warden's office became regular. He was brought there daily for the rest of the week, until it became unbearable for the two of them. Imad knew after a few days what the Warden would say, what he would do, and even where he would look.

He would take a Bic pen from the upper pocket of his jacket—he took it out.

He would tap the table with the back of the pen repeatedly—he tapped it.

He would pull off the pen's cover and secure it to the back of the pen—he secured it.

He would blow into his hands—he blew.

He would read the paper in front of him—he read.

The paper had the following written on it: "I, the undersigned, denounce the destructive Communist Party, and announce my loyalty and devotion to His Majesty the King and to his wise government."[11]

He would say, "Sign here"—he said it.

The Warden would throw his pen in frustration—he threw it.

He would drop his goatskin jacket off his shoulder—he dropped it.

He would walk toward the heater in the middle of the room—he walked.

He would throw his hat on the table—he threw it.

He would wipe his bald head with the palm of his hand—he wiped it.

He would go back and sit at the table—he sat.

"Oh God, how small his eyes were!"

Haj Mulqi, the prison warden, was a kind man.[12] He knew intuitively that the surrender of his prisoner and his signing of the statement would be a huge favor for the Pasha.[13] The Office of National Intelligence sent this case to the court. Why was he getting involved in this? Did he feel sorry for the boy? Perhaps the incentive behind this daily routine was to please the Pasha!

During these confrontations, the young inmate was not interested in defending what he thought was the most noble and complex ideology that had spread during the twentieth century. He was not thinking of Marxist and Leninist slogans. He was not worried about defending the platform of the Jordanian Communist Party. It was a daring game that could be summed up in two critical words: "Confess! Denounce!"

He found nothing to sustain him but a branch of jasmine and the story of *The Little Prince* to recall and occupy himself with. Stubbornness was a weapon that he enjoyed drawing. He used it this time to etch disappointment on the faces of his interrogators! He remained loyal to the scent of jasmine and felt an overwhelming joy when he dived more into his stubbornness.

Haj Mulqi returned to tapping the table with the tip of his pen in frustration. "Then, you will have to face the court."

". . ."

"It is a military tribunal."

". . ."

"Final. No possibility of appeal."

". . ."

"Ten years in exchange for signing under two lines!"

In the beginning, Haj Mulqi used to say each statement separately and wait for an answer; he then started to cut the time between the statements until he reached a point where he said them quickly as if they were a short, memorized rhyme: "Then you will be facing the court. The National Intelligence Court is a military tribunal with no chance of appeal. Ten years in exchange for signing two lines."

They allowed his father to visit him at the Detention Center. His father yelled at him, frustrated. "You are crazy, boy. You would let them imprison you for ten years for refusing to sign a two-line statement that will not add anything to His Majesty's positions or take much away from yours?"

Imad answered, "Father, I might be crazy as you say, but is the government crazy to jail someone for ten years on account of a two-line statement?"

The answer affected his father. He lowered his head and mumbled, "Screw this government."

The interrogator pretended that he did not hear that.

.   .   .

In a short time, Imad discovered the benefits of walking briskly in the prison courtyard. He grew accustomed to the sound of the nearby Catholic church on Sundays. He recognized the voices of the peddlers west of his ward changing their calls based on the products they were selling. He started listening to the sound of the drums and yodeling from the Women's Section behind the eastern wall, and he imagined them loose, attractive, almost naked, dancing . . .

He now had a space on the wall, ninety centimeters wide, to hang his belongings. His place on the floor extended one and a half meters. The inmates in the area where he was had to bend their legs when they slept at night in order to give some space to those who slept in the hallway between the East and West Sections.

Terms like *kanash*, *barsh*, *fawrah*, *gawoush*, and *mardawan* were words that remained from the time when the Turks brutally ruled the region. They continued to be common only in prison—as if prison had its own life that was not affected by time or paid no attention to change. The inmates in the hallway called the *Zogrut* were the common prisoners who had no power or influence.[14] They spent their time working with beads, weaving wool sweaters, and making long prayer beads from olive seeds.

Imad usually stayed up at night and slept during the day after the ward emptied so that he could stretch his legs. He saw strange things that people did in their sleep: snoring, sleepwalking, changing spots for strange reasons, and sleeping with their legs stretched up the middle column of the hallway. Right next to him slept two thieves in opposite directions, one's feet by the other's head. They were Abu Zahra and The Cat. Abu Zahra woke up, disturbed by The Cat's heavy breathing and uncontrolled trembling. He raised his head and asked sarcastically, "What's up?"

The Cat placed his foot on Abu Zahra's chest and pushed him away, saying, "Go back to sleep. Shame on you for spying on my dreams."

"Live and learn."[15] If it was not for Asaf, he would have had to sleep between the masses in the hall, but he was "lucky" because he was classified with Asaf as a third-class inmate. There were five classes of prisoners according to the Old Man's explanation:

- Furniture Inmates:[16] They were so called because their belongings, including their bedding, pots, pans, utensils, and food, were from outside the prison. These were the residents of the "White House," the selected elites. They were allied with the prison administrators and helped spread their rumors. They exercised self-control and followed orders.
- Trustees:[17] They were inmates trusted by the prison administrators to run the daily affairs of the prison, and they received favors in return for their service and loyalty. They occupied the corner of the ward and competed for one of the two windows to use as a closet (a valuable asset).
- Residents:[18] They were the inmates who occupied the four rows adjacent to the walls, like the shop owners, or who received financial support from their families, including Imad.
- *Zogrut*: They were the "proletariats" of the prison. They slept next to each other in opposite directions, bunched in the spaces around the bases of the large round columns of the hall. They were the first ones to wake up, and they slept right after having their evening meal. Some of them worked in the kitchen, cleaning, doing odd jobs, repairing broken items, making mats out of tattered blankets, and repairing broken kerosene stoves.
- Ambassadors: They were the temporary prisoners that sniffed fumes, got drunk, got into fights, and pickpocketed. They were usually picked up under "suspicious circumstances" without clear charges. They were constantly in and out of prison and had no particular place in the prison or outside it. That is why they were called ambassadors: they were always moving. They were housed in a designated place called the "embassy."

The station of the prisoners rose and fell with the influence of two other groups that were not included in the classification—the "birds"[19] and the "sloths."[20] The birds were the eyes of the administration and the many ears of the security apparatus. They were offended when called birds; they were present among all the five groups. So were the "sloths," who made a conscious decision to face the prison sentence with laziness, sleep, and ignoring life. They were present in every quarter, and among them was His Excellency, a former minister and a resident of the White House.

The inmates were counted twice a day: the midday count and the evening count. The midday count took place after lunch; the inmates stood in the courtyard in a line divided by groups of five and were counted. For the evening count, they stood, each over his mat, then, once counted, sat down. Counting was repeated if the number did not match what was on the official roster.

Officer Hayder came into the ward after the evening count. He walked by, inspecting the inmates sleeping in the pathway, and came to the area where Abu Haddid was. Imad was listening to the inmates compete in exaggerating the plots of their tales and glorifying their actions in an attempt to convince him to write down what they said. They were honest and tough, and when their stories became obviously exaggerated, they mocked this, laughed about it, and accepted it as part of the craft and magic of telling a good tale.

Officer Hayder interrupted their conversation and the chess game they were playing.

"Proud of your bishop, Abu Zahra?"

"No. It will be knocked down by the knight."

They laughed.

The guard took a paper and pen and walked toward the trustee of the ward and asked, "Your request, Abu Haddid—what are your needs?"

Abu Haddid asked, "What's up?"

"Our aunt, the government, is becoming loving and kind!" responded another inmate.

Hayder scolded them. "You don't like the government, losers?"

"Wonderful government, ha, ha, ha, ha."

"Who is as fortunate as we are? We have the police, security apparatus, judges, and the courts all watching out for our comfort. Ha, ha, ha."

"Our aunt, the government, feeds us for free."

"What do you mean by feed? Ha, ha, ha."

"And free health care."

"Aspirin and penicillin for all ills . . ."

The voices overlapped in roaring sarcasm. Hayder took his whistle out of his pocket as a warning sign and said, "Keep your doubts to yourselves. Honestly, I have orders to convey your requests to the administration."

"What? The Red Cross inspection is tomorrow?"

Abu Haddid, the trustee, took charge. "Your aunt, the government, is kind; it is asking for your requests. Why does this bother you?"

The guard pointed the tip of his pen toward Imad and said, "We start with the guest."

Imad answered with a seriousness he regretted. "Is this a prison? It is more like a holding stable . . ."

Asaf hurried to absorb the disapproval that was apparent on the guard's face. "I have requests, officer."

"What are they, Asaf?"

Asaf said, speaking in a formal tone, "You don't organize tourist outings for us."

Hayder laughed. The prayer beads scattered again.

"My salary is low."

"My shoes are tight, officer."

"My wife is asking for a divorce."

Officer Hayder became angry and said, "From this column on, you are all restricted from participating in the break tomorrow."[21]

From the hallway, the voice of a man who had been pretending to be asleep through the whole event responded sarcastically, "Have mercy. You denied us a walk on the shores of the Riviera . . ."

"You are awake, *nus-insais*?[22] Get up and put on a show."

The Cat got up and performed. The ward was silent and attentive.

The Cat approached, exaggerating his movements, and pointed to an imaginary bottle of cognac, then picked it up.

Boghous, the café owner, did not let the bottle go before he gestured to The Cat to pay. The Cat handed him a quarter of a dinar. Boghous took the quarter and gave him back two qirsh.

"Three qirsh!" The Cat said dramatically.

"When you return the bottle, you will get one back," said The Cat with an Armenian accent, imitating the café owner.

The Cat poured the imaginary contents of the bottle into his mouth, took a deep breath, shook his head, wiggled his hips, and licked his lips, screaming ecstatically, "Diesel!" He turned his face around, pretending to talk to Boghous, and said, "Don't give me back the qirsh. Give me a pickle." Then he added, "The

Cat ate the pickle and felt thirsty. Boghous demanded that he pay first. What will the poor Cat do?"

The inmates responded, "Ah. He steals."

"And what will the ever awake eye of the government do?"

"Imprison him."

"They lose sleep to take care of me! Ha, ha . . . as if there were no thieves in this city other than The Cat!"

This was the first time Imad had seen The Cat perform. He laughed whole-heartedly; it was the first time he had laughed in this place. The Cat brilliantly played all three roles—smoothly switching between Boghous with his Armenian accent and large belly, who constantly batted his eyelashes; the drunk customer; and the government.

Officer Hayder left laughing. "You are crazy, crazy!"

In the midst of all of the excitement, the officer forgot to tell Imad about the date of his court hearing, which was set for April 26, 1977.

The Trial

Apparently, the memory of pain is short.

Imad grew accustomed to Asaf's neatness, the agility of The Cat, the tattoos on Abu Zahra's arm, the thick lips of Abu Haddid, the silence of Suspicious, and the large nose on the Old Man. "Why do noses grow larger as people grow older?" he wondered.

The ticking of the clock became routine. Today is like yesterday and like tomorrow. Not much different from the way people live outside prison!

Imad forgot the scent of jasmine and became accustomed to the fleas, the morning sun, the water basin, the visiting screen that extended past the east entrance of the building, and the taste of burnt chickpeas in Tamouni's Café.[23] The café, less than a meter square, was the only luxury the inmates had. The cooking utensils hung on the wall, and the small space was just enough to provide its customers with tea, coffee, and loose Kamal cigarettes.

Imad bought two cups of coffee and a cigarette. He sat in a sunny corner with the Old Man, who was busy making a beaded necklace. The Old Man raised his tired eyes; his Adam's apple moved up and down on his wrinkled neck. He said, "What's going on, son? I see you're becoming accustomed to life in the stable."

He did not fully understand. He looked at the old face. The Old Man's keffiyeh with its black checks, which he wore even when sleeping, cast a shadow on his wrinkled cheeks, making them appear more sunken than usual. The Old Man reminded Imad of the foreman at the print shop of *al-Sabah* newspaper, where he had worked the previous summer. Just like his supervisor, Old Man always looked tired and weary.

Imad realized now that Old Man was still annoyed by his earlier comment that they were like animals in a stable. "Here is where your ancestors slept before they moved to Hawara.[24] Bedouins ruled then and no one lived on the plains. Do you know why?" Old Man asked.

Imad remained silent, but thought, "What's he talking about?"

Old Man continued: "They used to harvest their crops and store them in the dungeons and wells. They lived in the mountains. They took out their rations little by little, as needed, at night, secretly." Then he adjusted his keffiyeh and added, "That's how the farmers kept their food safe from Bedouin raids and Ottoman taxes.[25] Didn't your father and grandfather tell you?"

Imad knew what Old Man was referring to, but he did not fully understand. He wanted to know more. He scratched his head and was getting ready to inquire about his ancestors' relationship to the prison, called at the time Dar al-Saraya,[26] when Old Man's fingers stopped threading beads, and with his large nose pointed at the sky, he said, "Today, you see it as a prison, a stable. Animals become used to their bondage, but men cannot be chained!"

Imad did not know what to say, so he remained silent!

"Maybe I'm used to it. My time has passed. But you're still a young man at the beginning of your life. Stay alert!" Then the Old Man raised his head proudly and said, "I'm the son of the al-Tal family.[27] My house is on the side of the hill, the one next to Doctor Henawi's." He swallowed his tears and continued, "I feel like my house is so far away, as far away as the Northern Star. I'm used to prison life now."

Asaf's sudden appearance interrupted their conversation. With the arrogance of someone bearing great news, he announced, "There'll be no trial, cousin!"

Old Man laughed, wiped his big nose and tears with the corner of his keffiyeh, and said, "You submitted your reports and then showed up, Asaf?"

Asaf didn't pay any attention and went on talking to his cousin: "News from the source of the spring!"

Old Man raised his white eyebrows as his fingers skillfully carried on threading beads. Imitating Asaf's lisp, he said, "How do you know? From Officer Atalla?"

"Who's Officer Atalla?" Imad asked.

"Ignore that. This is directly from my uncle, the Pasha."

"The same Pasha that put you in prison, Pasha Said?"

Although the news of "no trial" intrigued Imad, he pretended not to care. Old Man was telling the truth; Asaf was a perpetual liar. His current two-year jail sentence was the result of him ripping off the Pasha. Asaf had visited the Pasha in the city and said to him, "Uncle, I admit I embarrassed you in the past, and I am sorry.[28] I am done with troubles. I want to grow up and become an honest man. Please help me get a good job where I can make a decent living."

The Pasha told him, "You have no degrees and no experience except your criminal record."

"But I truly want to straighten out my life."

"Look for a job in the market and prove yourself, then I will help you."

To avoid trouble, the Pasha had given Asaf ten dinars and sent him with his driver to the bus stop for Irbid. Asaf first asked the driver to stop at a fancy furniture store. He entered the store and pulled out a card, telling the owner, "I am so-and-so, my uncle is the Pasha, and here is my identification."

"What can we help you with, sir?"

"The Pasha is upgrading his household appliances. He needs a television, a washer, a refrigerator, and . . ."

Asaf dismissed the Pasha's driver. He loaded his spoils into a truck and drove off to sell them in the market!

Later, the Pasha received a six-thousand-dinar bill, and Asaf landed in prison.

Earlier, Imad had asked his cousin Asaf, "What did you sell it all for?"

"Two thousand."

"That was cheap."

"Not at all. That is how much it was worth wholesale. You don't know how greedy the merchants are."

"What did you do with the money?"

"I bought a Volkswagen—white, like a dove."

The idea of "no trial" continued to ferment in Imad's mind—no court!

He said to Asaf: "Let's walk."

Asaf walked with his cousin. "The news is confirmed, but not by the Pasha," Asaf whispered.

"By whom, then?" Imad asked.

"By the government."

"Which government?"

"Officer Atalla told me and asked me not to tell you, but . . ."

"Stop!"

Imad immediately left Asaf and walked back to Old Man. "Abu Muhammad, who is Atalla?" he asked.

Old Man laughed loudly and said, "Didn't I tell you?"

■   ■   ■

When Imad laid his head on the pillow that night, Asaf's news of "no trial" was still haunting him. The scent of jasmine filled his head as he imagined the pardon. He felt as though he were a free bird soaring above Yarmouk University.[29] He remembered his friends and the meals on the green. Their optimistic thoughts of freeing Palestine, Arab unity, social justice, his strong belief in the right to free expression, and the freedom to change flooded his mind.

Imad's daydreams took him back to the classes with his professors and classmates at the university. He recalled conversations during the night shift at *al-Sabah* newspaper when discussion was split between supporters and opponents of the Syrian army intervention in Lebanon after the start of the Civil War. They would drink coffee and smoke cigarettes until the first copies of the morning papers were out. Their arrival from the top floor triggered renewed elation and a sense of accomplishment in their young hearts. They carried the copies, hot off the press; searched eagerly to see their names in print; and walked proudly with the first light of day to the heart of the city. They would eat hummus, ful, and falafel, and drink tea on the sidewalk of Hashem's Café, sharing their talent of describing the waking city in detail.

Here and now, in prison, Imad was no longer occupied with big dreams of liberty and freedom. His feelings about being an agent for change, a part of a greater cause that connected him to freedom fighters around the globe, had subsided. Instead, he had become content with caring about the conditions of prisoners. He thought about his friends, the ones who had complained about going to classes and having to work the newspaper's night shift, and pitied them for not realizing the joy of sitting with a girlfriend on a dusty sidewalk. He wished he could let them know of the tremendous pleasure to be had from sitting under the outstretched grapevines in al-Sarihi's garden, which had become an open-air café for the university students.

He thought to himself, "Oh my female companions, how much time I wasted praising socialism and missing the opportunity to tell you how pretty you were!"

"How cruel it is to walk aimlessly around the prison grounds. How wonderful it was to wander in the streets of the capital at sunrise! How much I miss the jasmine at our house!"

He concluded his sighs with cruel and bitter questions: "Why am I here? Why are you there?"

·   ■   ·

Imad was awake when, after the dawn prayer, they called his name to prepare for the trip to the capital!

They prepared an impressive caravan to accompany him. He sat alone in the box, the prisoner's cage, with two wooden benches that would easily hold twenty to thirty people. In front was a police car with its siren on, and behind, a jeep with a cannon and a machine gun. The procession continued on its way to Amman.

The trial was faster than he had expected. Imad entered the courtroom where the lawyer, Adi Madanat,[30] was waiting for him. "They have your sentence ready, but I will try to defend you anyhow," Adi told him.

Shortly after, the Irbid director of Intelligence entered with two of his officers and sat in the front. Two men followed him and were seated in the witness section. A handsome officer with two stars on his shoulder and a smile on his face stood by a podium with a sign that read "Public Defender."

The officer stared at Imad. Staring straight into the opponent's eyes with a serious gaze is truly a Jordanian habit!

The public prosecutor repeated what the prison warden, Haj Mulqi, had told him many times over. The only difference was that the public prosecutor did not wipe his forehead with the palm of his hand as he delivered his statement. When he received no answer, he continued, "There is no need for your confession or signature. The court will decide."

Imad sat in the defendant's cage and heard a soldier with a red ribbon yell out, "Court!"

The three intelligence officers, the public prosecutor, his lawyer, and the two witnesses all stood. The two police officers guarding Imad remained standing. Standing beside him, they made what looked like a number ten—Younis, tall and skinny, Haydar, short and fat. Imad did not stand up because he didn't know that he had to.

The judge entered with two other judges, on his left and his right. They stood behind their podium. Meanwhile, Imad's lawyer waved his hands and asked him to rise, repeating: "Get up! Stand up!"

He decided not to stand up, thinking that old people do not understand our generation, and that providing explanations only exhausts young people.

Angry, the judge left the courtroom, followed by the other two members of the court. Then, the world turned upside down. The lawyer explained, the intelligence officer threatened, while the public prosecutor wiped his forehead and looked out of the window. Haydar begged Imad to obey court procedures. Suddenly Imad realized the gravity of what he had done, and his memory was filled with the intoxication of jasmine. He enjoyed being daring.

"Court!" The judge and his two companions entered the courtroom.

Again, Imad did not stand up.

Again, the judges left!

Imad enjoyed this game and became more determined to not stand up.

The case might be adjourned!

Finally, they found a solution. They took Imad out of the courtroom, and then the court clerk called "Court!" Everyone stood until the judges were seated under the shadow of a statue of a blind woman carrying the scales of justice! Then, after the rest of the people in court had taken their seats, they brought Imad in.

The public prosecutor said something about the grave danger of Communism; the Irbid director of Intelligence said something about flyers, books, and papers; the two witnesses, whom Imad had never seen in his life, stood up and gave testimonies confirming that he was a dangerous Communist. Imad's lawyer responded with mumbo jumbo about the law, the constitution, and the right to a fair trial. Then, the judge stared at him and asked the ultimate judicial question: "Guilty?"

Imad answered with confidence: "Not guilty."

"Case adjourned."

A week later, Imad was taken back to the capital. This visit lasted only a few minutes. In the name of the King, the judge delivered a sentence of ten years in prison, based on Article 92, *Fighting Communism,* a law placed on the books in 1953.

Imad felt as though he was playing a mysterious role in a theatrical production! He was excited about quoting from the book *The Little Prince*: "Those who dare to ask questions do not wait for answers."

He did not feel disturbed. He did not even think about the court sentence; it was as if the judgment did not concern him!

He laughed, wondering: "Am I sane?"

■   ■   ■

Perhaps the universe is not what it is, but what we perceive it to be. At noon, the caravan returned from the military court in Amman to the top of the hill in Irbid.

The return trip seemed shorter than the outward one. Spring was on its last legs. When Imad stepped out of the box, the bright sun blinded him. He rubbed his eyes with his cuffed hands and walked, surrounded by his guards. They passed a woman selling fruit and vegetables, green onions, okra, baskets of cardoons, and trays of ripe berries. Officer Haydar stopped by bundles of green chickpeas to taste a few while Younis grabbed a bunch of sweet white mulberries. The sounds of the vendors faded as they approached the police headquarters. The whole convoy climbed the exterior set of stone steps, which had no rails and led to the prison administration office on the upper floor, without having to go through the front gates.

Imad walked into the office, overlooking the city—it was as threatening and deceiving as The Cat had described. He immediately noticed the guard towers, or more accurately, the guard shacks: small blue faded wooden domes, barely able to protect the weary guards from the rain and the scorching sun. Dilapidated domes with old crumbling walls, rusty barbed wire, and guards consumed with boredom, nowhere to flee.

He saw a depressed-looking guard standing at the bottom of the steps, where pots were arranged behind him that had no plants or flowers in them. Perhaps a warden who loved keeping plants and flowers once ran the place, a hobby his replacements did not have.

How Imad longed now for the grapevine canopies at the entrances of the crowded Irbid homes, where women sat in courtyards and terraces ornamented with pots of basil, tubs of violets, and rows of fireweed, snapdragons, and coleus, with their multicolored, velvety leaves.

The upper rooms of the building were considered modern by comparison, with the living quarters below. The officer on duty escorted him in. Haj Mulqi, the prison warden, took off his goatskin coat and met Imad in the center of the room. "Welcome, son."

He ordered Imad's chains to be removed and invited him to sit on one side of the couch. In front of Imad sat a man in civilian clothes. Haj Mulqi then asked Imad, in the same manner as he would a highly respected guest, "How do you like your coffee?"

"Without sugar."

The man in civilian clothes stretched his legs and puckered his face, saying sarcastically: "It came and went. My goodness, ten years! That is how real men should be!"

Haj Mulqi fidgeted in his seat, appearing to disapprove of what the man had said. The man in civilian clothes leaned his tall body forward and opened his palm as if anticipating a gift. He stared at Imad and said, "You know that you were sentenced to ten years. This means that, if you live, you'll leave the prison when the salt land flowers."

The most beautiful thing about Haj Mulqi was his eyes, but he could never effectively use them to stare at others. Instead, he wiped his bald head with the palm of his hand. "What fault is it of your father, the Haj, that you should drag him into this with you for ten years?" he asked.

Imad's silent response had a copper ring to it.

"I am sad for your mother."

A bitter lump formed in Imad's throat. He swallowed it and held fast to his copper silence.

Haj Mulqi said: "The government is not crazy. Forget the court and the sentence. Any time you decide to change your mind, we are ready to listen."

Perhaps Imad was convinced by what Haj Mulqi had said, for he gathered his thoughts together and started a gentle dialogue with himself that might have led to him changing his mind! But the officer in gray trousers, green sweater, and brown jacket quickly added, "But remember, when the ten years comes to an end, we'll keep on after you and make your life miserable."

With that remark, the man woke the wolf inside Imad! He stared at him; it was obvious that he was challenging the officer.

Haj Mulqi raised his coffee cup, which was brought to him without a saucer, and carefully took a sip. "They wanted to transfer you to Central Mahata Prison in Amman," he said.

"To be with your party and Comrades," the plain-clothes officer said sarcastically.

Haj Mulqi took a long sip from his cup. "But I said you should stay here, close to your family . . ." After a short, cold silence, he continued. "Think about it, son. Our King's pardon is broad."

Imad saw a fresh drip of coffee down the side of the chipped coffee cup in front of him. He lifted the cup quietly; the bottom had left a black circle on the table's surface. The cup was as heavy as the coming ten years would be, but not only was he able to drink it, he even enjoyed its bitter taste!

He cleaned away the drip of coffee with his thumb and thought about making a thumbprint in the bottom of the cup.[31]

Should I put my thumbprint? Not put my thumbprint? Put it? I am not going to put it.

He avoided the chipped side of the cup and drank the rest of the coffee quietly, focusing his sight on the circle the cup had left on the wooden table.

The man in the brown jacket rubbed his hands together and left the room without touching his coffee, saying, "No hope."

Haj Mulqi let Imad finish his coffee, and then ordered him back to his cell.

For some reason, every opening had its own smell. The jasmine door closed, and in its place a rotten entrance appeared. The threshold of the prison was a small step between two worlds. In prison, the door becomes a guard, the guard a key, and the key a rival. The smallest key is the key to the handcuffs. The most dangerous keys are the smallest. They say: "His prison key is in his hands and when he wants to, he can leave—just recant and leave . . . all it takes is his signature on a piece of paper! A piece of paper!"

How heavy is this! Is this the key?

Keys in prison are not actually keys, but locks that rattle day and night and remind the prisoner that he is a prisoner. The key to his release is a piece of paper, and that constantly reminds him that he was once free. What a difficult equation!

Imad stood waiting at the sacred isthmus between the exterior gate and the inside screen to be registered as a convicted felon. This isthmus would disturb his coming nights with a metal lump that continually rolled from his throat to the bottom of his navel and back—until God ordained an act of destiny.

Three months, five days, and three hours had passed since Imad entered the prison gates for the first time. Before that, he had spent two months, twenty-one days, and nine hours in the chambers of the Intelligence Detention Center, all of which had passed like a sudden feverish night.

Imad awoke to the foul odor of the prison. Even on that memorable day when they had arrested him, with the wind whistling and the cold slamming the walls and stinging the bones, when they had pulled him out of bed, cuffed him, and thrown him in the Land Rover, even then he had not felt this kind of bitterness!

They had come for him at dawn. He had resisted with kicks and screams. His father came out in his nightclothes, holding his Kalashnikov and firing a warning shot in the air. A loud voice yelled out, "It's the Intelligence, the Intelligence." The village's early morning peace was interrupted by a round of fire from a heavy machine gun mounted on the back of a dark-colored Land Rover. Imad thought the gun was pointed at his father's chest. Terrified neighbors flocked in their nightclothes to see what was going on. His mother came out with her hair tousled and embraced him, blocking punches directed at him. They dragged him violently away from her. He clung to the jasmine bush by the entrance to the house. In the distance, a wolf howled.

They handcuffed Imad and threw him into the vehicle. A branch of jasmine was still in his hand. He waved it determinedly and shrieked like a wounded wolf, "Don't worry, Mother!" The scent of jasmine, embroidered with frozen dewdrop crystals, spread and filled his soul with a determination to resist.

On that spring day, standing at that isthmus between the outer and the inner prison gates, Imad felt a bitterness weighing heavily on the jasmine fragrance within him. His soul felt constricted by the presence of the cage, which he used to see from outside the prison gates on his way back and forth to school. He had always seen it—but then as a circus prepared for others.

"No. I will not get used to this bitterness, Old Man."

"I will not surrender to prison time and its monotony."

"I will denounce the Party and make my peace."

■   ■   ■

Full of grief, he returned to his mat, his cell, the courtyard, and his companions. They welcomed him warmly and enthusiastically, like a brother returning from work in the Gulf.

"Any news out there about an amnesty?"

"I don't know," Imad answered.

Stating the obvious, Abu-Haddid said, "Of course, there'll be a general amnesty on Independence Day."

Because he had been in Amman, Imad appeared qualified, in the other prisoners' eyes, to talk about amnesty—as if he had been to see the King himself!

Amnesty was a magical word around which Imad wove his dreams of freedom every day. Tales of amnesty have been recounted in prison cells since man first experienced prison. Their echo resonated in Imad's soul until he decided when to be saved.

"How narrow is life without hope!

"How narrow is prison without fantasy soothing its pains!"

Imad drank from the intoxicating cup of this illusion to ease the bitterness welling in his throat. When his mother and father visited him, he told them about the rumors of an expected amnesty that were circulating widely in the prison, and their faces lit up with hope!

The Comrade

The official verdict against him legitimized his affiliation with the Party! Officer Hayder happily described the spring trip from Irbid to Amman and the details of the trial. He commended the boldness of the Comrade as if he was the Comrade of Comrades! His language when addressing him had changed: "Where is the Comrade? The Comrade went. The Comrade came. Do you want to play chess, Comrade? Ask the Comrade."

Since then, Imad was known among the prisoners and the guards as the Comrade. He now had a title like all the other prisoners: Abu Haddid (Father of Iron), Abu Alganani (Father of Bottles), Abu Hijab (Father of the Veil), as well as Khityar (Old Man), Shakeek (Suspicious), Labies (Dresser), Tanbal (Lazy). Other titles acquired in prison were Kurzum (The Short), Shaeet (Arsonist), Masees (One Who Sucks), and The Cat, The Canary, and The Bat. The guards, the officers, and the prison warden also had titles: Hayder Kubeh (a type of appetizer made in the shape of little American footballs), Younis the Mateet (Stretch), Haj Mulqi Abu Farwa (Father of Fur), and Atalla Gafa al-Saj (the bottom of the frying pan). It is impossible to remember all the titles.

With support from Officer Hayder, the Comrade's status in the living quarters improved. His mat was assigned a respectable corner near the southeastern part of the hall. Further, Asaf started to plead for his help in carrying out his inexhaustible schemes. He also used his closeness to the Comrade to enhance his reports to the Security Services!

Imad became used to the melancholy of prison. The positive side of all this was that now he could stretch his legs when sleeping, and he had a pillow to sleep on and share his feelings with.

The fragrance of jasmine spread to his throat that night and made him feel guilty for the terror he had caused his mother and father on the night of his arrest. He felt sorry for the small library in their house later looted in search of Marx, Engels, Trotsky, Lenin, and Mao Zedong. They found nothing but *The Little Prince* under his pillow. The strange thing was that in his trial, they listed *The Sexual Revolution* by Wilhelm Reich and *My Struggle* by Hitler as evidence against him!

When his brother came to visit him, he angrily kicked the wire screen that separated them, shook his fist, and said, "I wish I was in your place." What could he tell his brother? The screen was a meter high and one-third of a meter wide, topped with iron bars that stretched up to the ceiling. There was only enough space between the bars to allow one hand to reach in for a handshake. He held his brother's hand in silence.

His brother was a Baathist from the Salah Jaddid group. His passport was confiscated, and he was banned from public jobs, but fortunately, he found work in a private engineering firm that provided him sufficient income—better than a government job. For his political affiliation, his brother was disliked by the ruling Syrian Baath Party, the Iraqi Baath Party, and the National Intelligence Office controlling Jordan.

His father used to say, "What, an orphan party? It has no luck with the master, nor with the mistress!"

After Imad's arrest, his father frequently told his older brother, "I complained about the bad luck of one, to end up with the worst luck of another."

The brother bowed his head in despair and mumbled, "My mother started forbidding us from bringing books to the house!"

The brother noticed a former colleague, the Engineer, an inmate in the White House, and asked him to take care of Imad. The brother left realizing that his situation was much better than Imad's and that many other Comrades, hundreds affiliated with opposition parties, and thousands loyal to Palestinian organizations, were in worse situations than he was. Faced with restricted travel and banned from certain jobs, made living difficult for him, but at least he was not behind prison bars.

When the brother left, Imad thought, "Is it just a throw of the dice that cast me into this dismal place? Prison is a legal complicity between the authorities and society." Then he recalled, "According to The Cat, 'prison is a double standard!'"

· ■ ·

Life in prison is narrower than life outside, but it is crowded too. Here, they count beads, move chess pieces, throw dice, and calculate the repetitive footprints of time over their skin.

The limitedness of space in prison is a flat, primitive feeling. The prisoner misses things that people do not pay attention to in their daily lives. He rejoices like a child about things that are considered ordinary.

"When sleeping, isn't there pleasure in stretching my legs to the fullest extent?"

"How sweet it is to recall the fragrance of jasmine at the entrance of our home."

The fragrance of jasmine spreads with its astonishing simplicity. His mother's presence with her thick braids, dangling like a lifeline, appears.

"Mother, my soul flutters like a plucked bird, yearning for your warmth."

Imad yearned for her voice and recalled her stories at bedtime when she helped him overcome his fear.

"Once upon a time, there was a Haddidwan, and there was a ghoul . . ."

"Her teeth? How were her teeth, mother?"

"From the beginning, mother."

"Oh, we already said that."

"By the name of Saint Sharhabil, from the beginning, mother."

"From the beginning is difficult; where did we stop?"

"When the ghoul moved to the village."

The flame of the lantern flickered in its globe, and his mother continued: "The people fled the village and left it to the ghoul. No one remained in the field except Haddidwan. The ghoul followed Haddidwan, cornered him in an alley, and attacked him. He fled and she followed him, shaking the earth beneath her feet. He hid in the ironsmith's shop. The ghoul's large hand blocked the door. He banged on the walls with determination. Suddenly, the ghoul let out a scream that shook the empty village, and Haddidwan fell down terrified.

What a surprise! He saw the hand of the ghoul shrink and pull back quickly in fear of the fire."

"The ghoul is scared of fire!"

"He picked up a piece of wood and lit it, but the ghoul escaped. Haddidwan carried his lit torch and walked in the empty streets of the village as he pleased. When the sun rose, the ghoul hid in her dungeon.

"Haddidwan stood at the top of the wall and yelled, 'O People, the ghoul is scared of light and fire.'

"Haddidwan started to work in the daytime to gather his food and build a fire that protected him from the ghoul at night. He stood on the wall of the village every morning and called on whoever accidently came close to the wall, to come in and not fear the ghoul, but the villagers had already spread the fear to everyone they met.

"One day, a pretty, brave girl passed by and heard Haddidwan call. She stood by the gate and greeted him. Haddidwan was elated and said, 'Come, let us get married and have girls and boys and expel the ghoul.' The ghoul took advantage of the wedding celebration and ate everything in the village that would burn.

"Haddidwan was very angry, and yelled to the people outside the village wall to give him wood to rekindle his fire at night, but the people outside the wall were busy crying and preparing food for the ghoul."

"Why are they feeding her, mother?"

"The fear . . ."

"Why isn't Haddidwan afraid?"

She yawned. "Oh listeners, should we tell or sleep?"

"Tell, mother, tell; the desert of the night is endless."

Imad picked up the square wooden board that he used as a table for coffee and tea, and placed it on his knee, ready to write. Facing the wall, he sat cross-legged, held the pen in his hand, and wrote, "Haddidwan did not scare me. I fear. I feared that I would not return to my mother, and I did not return! I feared the nylon string, but it became a memory. If I knew what suffering awaited me, perhaps fear would have defeated me! I used to fear prison, and here I am in prison! But I'm not Haddidwan. I am not a hero."

He thought, "Miserable is the homeland that needs heroes." More crossed his mind: "I am not sure who said this beautiful thing. Does my homeland need heroes? The radio announcer said that my homeland is 'an oasis of security, stability, and is one family.' Is my country happy that I am in prison?

"The Intelligence Service is happy with me in prison, the Party is happy about where I am, and my friends are happy because I didn't tell on them. My country is very happy without me! But my mother isn't happy. I do not want to become a hero. I only want to live like the rest of God's creatures. Damn the Party, damn the government, damn the friends. I will confess, denounce, and—"

The Cat crawled between the sleeping bodies and rested his chin on the edge of the bedding. Imad was startled. "What, Cat?"

"Your problem, Comrade, is that you are not able to turn the prison into a joke and ignore it."

Imad hid the paper he had written in the palm of his hand and said, "Spare me your philosophy, Cat."

"Prison is a terrible joke."

"Fine. Fly away from here, Cat. I would like to sleep."

The Cat disappeared, and Imad remained stretched out on his mat, his eyes staring at the dome of the ceiling. He talked to his pillow about his plan to recant; she frowned and listened to him until he fell asleep.

In his dreams, he saw the "recantation" paper taking the shape of a doorstep at the prison entrance—about an inch high. He crossed to the outside, but found himself back inside. He woke up repeating the scenario in his mind.

He cried until his pillow was wet.

Imad became used to the company of The Cat. He had a sweet presence and slept less than the rest of the inmates, but when he slept, he saw dreams enough to last for two to three months. He saw bright, heavenly, fairy dreams. He always woke up smelling a divine fragrance. Soon, the scent from the kingdom of his happy dreams spread to those around him. Imad put his book aside and smiled at The Cat. "Come. Tell."

"In my dream, I saw the deer of dew, up with the light of dawn. They asked me, 'Where are you heading?'

"I said, 'To Qaisalah.' They took me with them. On the way, we woke the sleeping poppies, left morning greetings at the Valley of the Guards, sprayed the seedlings of oleander with dew, and passed by the tent of the gypsy. I carried her in my arms and flew with her to the mulberry tree. The gypsy said, 'Leave me; I want to sleep.'

"I said to her, 'Let me quench my desire for you; then you're welcome to go back to sleep.'"

"Were you satisfied?"

"My needs can't be fulfilled."

Imad laughed and asked, kidding, "What are your needs?"

The Cat's eyes twinkled with a deep yearning and said, "I want everything—just everything."

Imad laughed. "Just!" And he thought: "This just . . ."[32] A raging flood of desires rushed into his soul and did not stop. He himself had not known that he had all these desires.

He sighed and said to The Cat, "Tomorrow, I will be released."

"How?"

"I will denounce the destructive Communist Party. That is it."

"Is it destructive, Comrade?"

The Comrade laughed and said, "Not really. It neither builds nor destroys."

Imad respected his Party and liked his Comrades. While at the university, he strongly defended its principles, its leaders' positions, and was proud of its heroic sacrifices in Palestine and Jordan. Here, no one cared about his views.

He was always a good reader, a dreamer. His dreams inspired his drawings, and Abu Musa, his Party leader, was not only his mentor, but he also looked at his drawings, read his writings, supported him, and shaped his thinking. His newfound ideology pulled him together and gave his paintings, readings, dreams, and reflections a deeper meaning, vitality, and radiance. It all became connected to something bigger than himself.

In the Intelligence Detention Center, he did not think of any of this. He did not recall the theory of Historical Materialism or Surplus Value. He recalled the tale of *The Little Prince*, from which he borrowed images for his paintings that impressed his colleagues.

(If somewhere we do not know, there was a sheep that we do not know, what difference does it make to us if it did or did not eat a rose? None of the adults would understand.)

The Cat understood me.

.   .   .

The Cat was truly a cat! He was not handsome or important, but when he returned from his work in the evening, his lightheartedness was contagious and transformed the ward, filling it with a cheerful atmosphere. He entertained them with folksongs and tales.

When The Cat was absent from the wards, melancholy spread to Imad's and the other inmates' souls.

"Where could The Cat be?"

"The guards frequently punish him and place him in solitude."

"What would he have been punished for?"

"Because he had snuck into the forbidden zone by the exterior gate."

This was not the first time The Cat was missing from the ward; nevertheless, Imad missed him.

He kept himself busy with a paper and a pen, drew "the bird and the cage," the most basic and profound picture throughout history, well known to children. He pushed the bird's head out of the cage, his wings stretched, tearing the wires.

The Cat said one evening, during one of his frequent satiric performances, "The origin of man is not a monkey. It is a soul with two wings; when you discover your soul, its wings will grow!" Now Imad was giving the idea serious consideration.

He continued to stare at the drawing without adding a line. He missed the fragrance of jasmine and thought about getting two wings to fly away from the pungent smell lingering in this gloomy prison.

"Should I denounce the Party and declare my loyalty to the 'wise government'?"

He laughed desperately. "If only they had not imprisoned me.

"Why didn't I do it the first day?

"What would The Cat and the Old Man think of me?

"Would I betray the jasmine bush?

"Would I let down my sister, who brags about me relentlessly?" Then he thought, "Abu Musa, my Comrade who held firm against the oppression of Zionist occupation in Palestine, my colleagues at the university, my brother, my father, and my mother—what would they think?

"I would betray my soul and would not be able to grow wings as long as I lived."

Imad felt the branch of jasmine spread its roots into his soul, and saw the step by the exterior gate rise up to his reach.

"What would be easier: bearing a restricted, shattered life, or enduring the wards with their intense, steamy, foul odor?"

He could not sleep that night.

■ ■ ■

Imad was the first to arrive at Tamouni's Café that morning, alone, drinking his black coffee, and searching in the sky for a space large enough to encompass his dark, gloomy questions. The small space in the horizon over the prison had tattered edges. It was a separate space—not a piece of the city's wide sky, but a cheap patch randomly placed there.

The limitedness of space provoked the question of time. Time was a lantern, oil was its movement, and wick its accomplishments. Even heaven was unbearable without accomplishments.

The Cat arrived, interrupting his thoughts and spreading joy. He stretched his arms, welcoming the half sun peeking over the wall, took a deep breath, and ran his long fingers through his soft, long hair. With his face lit, his features became more defined: bright eyes, thin face, large flat nose, wide mouth, thick lips. Two crescents formed on the side of his face when he smiled. His ears stood like stiff feathers, and his nose trembled, craving a hot, sweet cup of tea.

Imad ordered him a cup of tea.

The Cat drank it with pleasure.

Officer Hayder approached, rattling his keys and scolding, "Come Cat, don't waste time."

The Cat picked up his bag of tools from the inventory officer by the interior gate and went to work. He worked as a plumber: he repaired faucets, opened clogged sewage, and fixed broken pipes. This allowed him to go beyond his ward and sneak out by the exterior gate at sunset to enjoy the sight of the city descending from the top of the hill toward Palestine Street before slowly stretching upward to the south in the direction of the tree nursery and Yarmouk University. At the end of the long street, he could see with his inner eye his city, Irzala, resting by the mulberry trees where the poppies covered the grass with dark, ruby red.

In the evenings, the inmates gathered around The Cat, waiting to hear his tales. He recalled the scene as if he were free in Irzala, eating his breakfast under the mulberry tree, looking out over the Valley of the Guards with its lush green grass. He described the springs flowing under the moonlight with shimmering silver water. He filled their lungs with fresh air, awakened their senses. He took them to camps where gypsies roamed and songs rang loud and sweet, and said, "They passed by alone, with no chaperones, walking slowly, step by step, over the dewdrops, spreading joy." Then added, "Oh, how we danced and sang all night; I would make love to her and shower her with gifts and riches." He would then end his story, laughing, "Ha, ha, ha. Don't ask me where I got the money from."

Imad said, "Oh God, he was born to be free and sing. It is unfortunate that he was a thief and that he is in prison." The Cat sat silent, feeling grateful for what Imad said. Then, gradually, he gave in to grief, crawled onto his mat, and fell asleep.

Karma

mad's friendship with The Cat grew. That angered Asaf. He objected to The Cat and Abu Zahra joining their circle. Their close, small group prepared dinner and ate together, and Asaf didn't want those two to be part of it. "Abu Zahra, I can understand," Asaf said. "He can wash the dishes and light the Primus stove. But The Cat—a plumber—that repulses me."

Old Man rubbed his large nose. "Cleaner than you," he said to Asaf.

Asaf didn't give up and whispered to the Comrade: "Cousin, you don't know The Cat. If you ask me, he's a bastard, a limb cut off a tree, with no important relatives to back him up and no followers."

Imad interrupted him. "Come on, Asaf. There are more prisoners here who are sons of tribesmen and important clans than there are bastards!"

"The Cat is a lazy snitch. He cannot keep a secret. Tomorrow you will see, and say, Asaf said so."

▪   ▪   ▪

Asaf was a smart, handsome, witty, and imaginative young man. In prison, he gained the nickname of Sharp Dresser. He dressed neatly, and his shoes were always shining. His lisp made him sound almost aristocratic and inspired trust in his listeners. When he was young, Asaf lisped, pronouncing the letter "r" as a "y." Then he discovered that the sound "*gh*" was more flexible, softer on the ear of the listener, and had its own charm. His God-given talents were employed to trick people. He was a scheming swindler and a skillful liar.

He was also an informer. This made the self-appointed guard, Abu Haddid, tolerate Asaf's objections to accepting The Cat in the elite group. Of course, they were the elite of only the South Ward. The Cat was a "bird" who sang to the guards without hesitation whatever he saw and heard. But Imad forgave The Cat these trivial transgressions, such as telling that "so-and-so has a knife, so-and-so smuggled hashish into the northern side of prison, the shop of so-and-so sells *agho . . .*"

The Cat laughed whenever Imad drew a caricature of him with a black bandana, a chain with large keys hanging from his waist, and a screwdriver in his left hand (for he was left-handed)! The Cat curled his fingers to make a half circle, turned the picture around, and said, "I only turn the door knob or push the window, and if it opens, I go in."

"And if it doesn't open?"

"To hell with it." (He actually used a profane word.) "Others will open it."

Prison is a comfortable refuge for thieves. In prison, they take a break from work. No theft had been reported against The Cat, Abu Zahra, or their companions in prison. However, thieves have the highest rate of prison escape, aided as they are by their ability to infiltrate and their experience in unlocking locked doors.

Abu Zahra was a modest petty thief who stole from entryways and porches. He stole laundry, slippers, plants—and even a flower from a garden! In prison, he was the most skillful at self-mutilation and cutting with a razor, in addition to his skill at playing chess. He moved a pawn on the chessboard and told Imad, "One spring, The Cat escaped from prison to steal, and in the winter, after spending all his money, voluntarily returned, turning himself in to the police after sorting through their long list of stolen items." Then he added, "The Swimmer, the most renowned thief in Jordan, escaped more than once, and from more than one prison. But he spent his retirement, until he passed away, playing dominoes in Amman's Central Prison."

The Comrade moved his bishop, threatening Abu Zahra's king with what he thought was a fatal move, and asked The Cat about the escape incident. The Cat looked embarrassed, his face turning red, and he stuttered, "That was a long time ago. Forget it."

"Checkmate."

Abu Zahra won the game by protecting his king with a knight and trapping Imad's king. Without gloating, he continued his story: "The Cat is smart. He pretended he was suffering from pain in his right kidney, and kept going to see the doctor and describing the classic symptoms of having a gallstone until the doctor referred him to hospital. He taped a pebble to his side, which appeared in the X-ray in the middle of his kidney. The hospital admitted him, and he escaped through a hospital bathroom window!"

The thieves were loyal to one another and talked with respect about each other. Class did not exist among thieves. They treated one another with an astonishing equality, regardless of their level of education, of their professions, prospects, or specialization. Thieves did not brag about their lineage or education. Education was not necessary for that profession; it did not give a thief any favorability at all. Status was based on experience, which they all freely shared. They knew the laws pertaining to their profession better than the judges.

State officials caught embezzling were denied the title of thief because, according to The Cat, "They work and have a monthly salary, and their stealing is a secondary job that they do out of greed, abjectness, and lowliness."

∎ ∎ ∎

That evening, The Cat was different. He did not sing or recall the details of his day in his usual theatrical manner. When his companions asked him, as they did every evening, "Come on! Tell us. What did you see today?" he replied, "Nothing," and went to sleep!

Shortly after midnight, The Cat woke up and saw Imad sitting cross-legged on his mat. He crawled close to him. "Are you awake, Comrade?" he asked.

Imad chided him gently. "Spare me your dream, Cat."

"Not a dream, Comrade. It's something that actually happened."

"You tell all your dreams as if they actually happened."

"I have something that I can't tell anyone but you," he whispered determinedly.

"Tell it to the police records."

The Cat grew anxious, showing a deep sadness that curled inside him. Comrade Imad felt sorry for him, sat up straight, sighing, and said, "Please tell me."

The Cat whispered hastily, "Yesterday, I went into the women's prison."

He waited for a smile to indicate that the Comrade was listening, and continued. "As usual, Madam Malika had sent the prisoners to their rooms and gone back to her office. At the bathroom door, the guard unlocked my handcuffs."

Imad stretched out his legs, crossed them again, placed his hand under his chin, and listened to The Cat. "The pleasure comes, Comrade, when I recall what happened. When I was there, I had no time to process what was happening. I was consumed with pleasure. I do not know how to explain it to you. But the true pleasure comes later, when you repeat the film."

"What film? I do not understand what you are saying. Speak slowly."

"I went to the bathroom to clear the clogged drain. When I opened up the access, a sour stench came out. I'm used to it, but the guard closed the bathroom door and lit up a cigarette. I asked him to leave it open—the smell of the urine was suffocating—but he refused, saying, 'And you smell like cologne?'"

"No problem. I found myself alone in the bathroom where the women bathe. In the corner was a Primus stove roaring away with a pot of water boiling on top of it. The steam filled the room. On the other side of the room was a low wall with a plastic curtain draped above it. It moved. I rubbed my eyes to see and I saw a woman standing behind the half wall. First, a nipple flashed in front of me. I thought I was dreaming and went up closer. She was frightened and hid behind the wall. I went even closer, and I saw! . . . I saw her hair loose, black, and falling around her face. She was dripping with water, her chest was full, and her nipples stood like berries. I became dizzy and almost fell down. I looked shocked. I wanted to tell her, 'I am here to check the drainage.' But she was smarter than me. She stood up, placed her finger to her lips, and whispered, 'Alone?'"

"My hand involuntarily reached out and stroked her skin. When I peered at her behind the curtain, her chin trembled. Her wet lips touched mine, and I felt a sting. I sank into them. She was boiling over, her body soft and warm, like a melting peach. She was in her thirties, or maybe forty—who cares? Her hair was soft and long, and her eyes laughed. She opened like a flower. Nothing was left in my head except the smell of her soap and the whooshing sound of the Primus stove.

"Desire wrapped everything in its sweetness. I held her and she did not resist. The plastic curtain fell between us; she stretched out her hand and removed it. Softly, she stroked it. It stiffened. She kneeled and placed it in her mouth. Her neck was a cone of sugar, her ears could be munched on, and her lips satisfied my hunger. She stood up. Our legs wrapped around each other. We slipped, and I was on top of her—nothing between us except the lather of the soap, bubbling. The soap and sweat on her skin were honey and butter. Her chest by itself was enough to fill my dreams until the end of time. Her back was a meadow, and her belly like that of a cat, fuller from the belt down. When I thrust into her, it was warm, melting, like a piece of *gatayef* drenched in honey—close and far, deep and delicious.[33] She held me tight and swayed. I screamed and Karma gasped. Our honey gushed and the bathroom turned to a love roller coaster.

"The whooshing of the Primus stove subsided, and we melted in the foam. I pulled myself into her lap and started shaking. She pulled her damp abaya that had been tossed in the corner of the bathroom over us, and I fell asleep. I slept as if there were no guards at the door or female jailers in the courtyard. I forgot them, I forgot the jail, and I forgot you. It was only she, I, and the smell of our sweat. I felt safe. She whispered, 'What's your name?' I told her, 'Saeed, but they call me The Cat.' She laughed. 'A Cat?'

"The Primus stove died. The cloud of desire subsided, and the smell of the kerosene mixed with the stench of urine spread again. She gathered up her clothes and hid behind the door. I opened it. The sun blinded me, and I remembered that I was in prison! I blinked and her image flashed back and forth in my mind.

"'Did you get your whole body in the sewage?' the guard asked.

"'All good?' Malika Khanum asked.

"I said nothing. I did not even feel the handcuffs when the guard placed them on my wrists. I picked up my tools and left. Nothing was in my head but her image. If I could draw like you, I would draw her in full. Even the mole by her armpit, the birthmark below her navel, and the scar from the smallpox vaccination on her arm. But there is something that cannot be drawn, Comrade—her fragrance. How is that? Better than incense and basil is the scent of her skin. Doesn't each of us have his own smell? Hers is different. How? I do not know. It is trapped in my head and cannot be erased."

• ■ ■

The story of Karma and The Cat spread through the prison. Imad swore to The Cat that he wouldn't reveal his secret.

The Cat put a reassuring hand on the Comrade's shoulder. "Shit! I do not care. Ha, ha, ha . . ." he said, laughing.

The prisoners whispered the story to each other, filling in the missing details. The story was told in many different ways. Each added his own experience to the tale. The versions varied to the point of contradiction, and this became the favorite narrative, told by all, with each producing a scenario that pleased him.

Only Abu Haddid continued to say, "The story of Karma is just a lie from start to finish, one of The Cat's imaginary tales."

Karma became the object of endless inmate dreams, except for poor Abu Zahra.

Imad moved his white knight to the middle of the chessboard; Abu Zahra moved nothing.

"What are you daydreaming about, Abu Zahra?" Imad asked.

Abu Zahra's eyes were filled with tears, and he whispered, "Last night, I had a wet dream, Comrade."

Imad laughed. "Karma?"

"I wish!"

"A boy?"

The words stuck in Abu Zahra's throat. He forced them out. "I dreamed that I was thrusting."

"What's wrong with that?"

Abu Zahra wept. Imad gathered up the chess pieces and went with Abu Zahra for a walk in the prison courtyard. Abu Zahra told Imad about how he grew up listening to his mother's complaints during the day and to her moans at night. She died giving birth. When he grew up, his father killed his sister because someone had slept with her!

Abu Zahra had never had sex with a woman or anyone else. He considered it harmful to the other partner; he would not hurt an ant. The poor man's aggression was limited to cutting himself with a razor when he became angry, and his sexual experience was confined to masturbating.

"When you masturbate, what do you fantasize about, Abu Zahra?"

He wiped a tear from his face and said bitterly, "A female donkey, or a cat, or a horse . . ."

▪   ▪   ▪

Karma became the secret code that the prisoners used to conceal the story from the prison authorities. She was a secret they all kept, despite the many whistleblowers, informers, and spies with loyalties to Central Intelligence, the Prevention Unit, National Security, and Narcotics. Imad did not share this with the Party. The Cat's status rose. He and his companion, Abu Zahra, joined the elite group and started eating with them at the same table.

"Bastards!" Asaf whispered angrily.

Abu Haddid appeased him. "All men are bastards and each covers his sins in his own way." Asaf pretended to agree. Imad was terribly disturbed by the assertion!

The Denouncement

I t was a pleasant summer day. Hopes were high for a royal amnesty in celebration of Independence Day. Their hopes for possible release became stronger when, one day, after the daily count, the loud speakers announced the names of 142 "ambassadors" detained without a charge, instructing them to collect their belongings and gather at the main entrance. With the release of one fourth of the inmates, the hallways were less crowded, and the prisoners' spots changed. Some rose to a better location, and others enjoyed stretching their legs all the way when sleeping. Nothing happened during the following three days, and their anticipation of a royal amnesty vanished. This left the prisoners depressed and consumed by a deep feeling of injustice, as if they had been sentenced all over again.

The Comrade was very disappointed that night, as if he had already been granted the royal amnesty and lost it. His mind was occupied with endless questions, a constant search for answers. By the time the sun came up that morning, he had made up his mind. He told himself, "Just as I confronted the interrogation and its consequences, I can handle the confession and its consequences."

He wrote his confession and denouncement of the Party in the middle of a white page with beautiful script. He then wrote his full name, signed it, placed both the Gregorian and Hijri dates under the signature, and went to sleep content.

He woke up midday when he heard the whistle for the day count, pulled out the paper he had written, read it, and placed it back in his pocket. He convinced himself that working hours were almost over and that he should postpone the matter to the next day.

In the afternoon, The Cat returned from his work, washed, and walked toward Tamouni's Café, laughing.

"Why are you in a rush as if you are on your way to bury someone?" they asked him.

The Cat laughed and said, "We buried the amnesty rumor!"

The Old Man said, "As if you are better than the rest of us to get it, twig!"

"Me?" asked The Cat, laughing. Then he drank his tea in large gulps, walked quietly to the exterior gate as he did every evening, and looked far into the open and wide space beyond the gate.

How beautiful was Irbid, surrounded by its villages like a necklace. Hanging gardens, crimson roofs, walls of fig and olive trees, and a sea of wheat. Fresh air, clouds, dewdrops, and green as far as the eye can see.

The guards caught The Cat by the exterior gate and sent him to the dungeon for punishment. The Comrade pleaded for his release with the prison warden, Haj Mulqi.

The Break

The bitter experience of the past becomes sweet if written with the ink of the present. Time stretches under the stress of isolation and appears short if you hold it in the palm of memory. Time is like water; it takes the shape of the place.

The days stretched and the nights seemed shorter. Imad became accustomed to the voice of the muezzin at Mameluke Mosque in the morning and the tolling of the bells at the Catholic church on Sundays. He got used to standing in line in a group of five for the midday count and sitting and standing for the evening count. His mother's visits became regular and summer vacation approached. He no longer watched high school students pass by the prison on their way to and from school. The women farmers arrived outside the prison walls with their fresh produce of cucumbers, peas, and okra. He heard their voices fighting with older men for the space the men monopolized by the west side of his window. He could hear them call, "watermelon, cantaloupe, figs." He heard the officers from the municipality frequently argue with the farmers, collect fees, and close the stands when they refused to pay. The sun continued to rise and set every day, and the Comrade continued to go over the confession paper every night, then place it back in [his pocket], as if he was waiting for a special occasion to hand it in.

After the counting ritual, the inmates gathered around the dinner mat. Abu Zahra cleaned his mouth with the palm of his hand and said, "We finished dinner and the sun has not set yet!"

Abu Haddid stared at him while chewing his food and making a noise that sounded like the footsteps of a man walking in mud. The Old Man held the bite that he was about to put in his mouth and said, "They promised to extend the break period until evening prayer. Haj Mulqi himself promised us that during the visit of the Red Cross delegation."

While carefully gathering the last food crumbs on his plate, Imad added, "All guards care about is to finish counting so that they can lock us up and go early to rest. Meanwhile, we are cooped up in here like chickens."

Suspicious added with his faint voice, "How come they do what they want? Are we their slaves?"

Asaf pulled a tissue out of his pocket and said, "If the Warden promised, the guards should obey."

Abu Zahra commented while collecting the olive pits and the empty plates, "The judge and prosecutors are one; what can we do?"

Imad said, "Tomorrow evening, when they ring the bell, we will not go in."

Asaf whispered, "Hush, you don't want someone to hear this, cousin. This is rebellion; they will shoot us."

In the morning, when Imad went out to drink his coffee with Old Man at Tamouni's Café, the prisoners were smiling at him, including those that he barely knew. The leaders among them walked by, making fists and raising their thumbs in encouragement. Apparently, Asaf's "Hush" quickly reached the prison administration: "The Comrade says, 'no one should go in in the evening.'"

The rumor spread like fire!

Everyone was curious. The prisoners walked around nervously and looked at each other with eyes full of questions and anticipation. The guards carried their batons, acted harsh, and forced those who had been excused in the past to get in line for the midday count. Even the residents of the White House had to come out to the courtyard and stand in line. This increased the prisoners' agitation and revealed their frustration.

Imad anticipated trouble, and his knees trembled.

When the roll-taking finished, he asked to meet Haj Muqli in an attempt to avoid the worst.

The officer on duty told him abrasively, "The Haj is on vacation; what do you want?"

The vein beneath his throat pulsed, waking the "wolf" in him.

His anticipation reached its zenith, and he snapped, "None of your business."

Officer Atalla was taken aback and said with a softer tone, "I am acting as warden; if you have something, say it to me."

This critical moment is confusing, like a spark that glimmers with the voice of a faraway wolf and quickly disappears after it ignites the soul with an obsession that makes all calculations and anticipations vanish, leaving behind a charged moment, dripping with a unique intoxication.

Imad felt more determined than ever, and said sternly, "Thank you," and walked away.

Officer Atalla was taken by surprise, and he thought, "Since most of the prisoners collaborate with me, the ones who do not must be collaborating with someone else. This boy's uncle is the Pasha; perhaps he is cooperating with someone who is higher than me." He further thought, "Perhaps this is what spared the Comrade from further interrogation and severe punishment!"

When the evening bell rang, Imad and Shakeek were walking around the courtyard, as inmates usually do. Shakeek asked with his naturally low voice, "Should we go in, Comrade?"

Imad answered instinctively. "No one goes in."

The comment spread as if it concerned the inmates collectively and each of them individually.

When Imad said what he said, nothing had been decided; but the minute Shakeek asked, it became a done deal.

The prison became quiet, and the usual clattering of the plastic tables and chairs at Tamouni's Café stopped. The inmates poured into the courtyard. Even those who were inside the prison preparing their evening meals came out.

Officer Atalla repeated his call through the loudspeakers. "Ward trustees, get the prisoners in."

The five sections of the prison echoed the guards' whistles. They announced the end of the break. The trustees ordered the prisoners back to their wards, but the prisoners refused to go in!

The prison's emergency bells were sounded. The lead guards of the five wards entered the courtyard and closed the interior gate of the prison behind them.

Meanwhile, the machine guns mounted on the prison wall were redirected to the courtyard, and police officers appeared on the rooftops with their weapons drawn.

Imad became more nervous and yelled, "Emergency!" Meanwhile, Shakeek continued walking, ignoring the fear that spread around him. A yodeling came from the women's prison. A repeated call from the loudspeakers asked the prisoners to return to their wards immediately.

The inmates were excited. They filled the prison courtyard, as if they had come from outside the prison. They heard a voice calling, "A sit-down protest, a sit-down protest!" It was the voice of Comrade Imad.

Shakeek responded, directing his comment to all who were at the courtyard. "We will not go in until after the Maghrib call to prayer."

Kurzum, the trustee of the North Ward, stood at the edge of the water fountain and said enthusiastically, enunciating his words and raising his arm with its tattoo of a spotted snake, "This is an unacceptable reaction. I promise Comrade that we will not go in, even if they shoot us."

The Cat turned to a group of prisoners congregated at one corner of the courtyard and asked loudly, "Guys, no one should go back in?"

A woman sent a loud yodel from the women's prison. Abu Zahra ripped his undershirt, exposing a hairy chest full of scars, and the *Zogrut* took out their blades and exposed their tattooed arms in a clear declaration that they were ready to cut themselves if the police attacked!

Imad's nervousness subsided when he saw the inmates' response. Everyone was in the courtyard. Even Transistor, Canary, and Pipe came out of the White House and sat at the edge of the fountain. Then Hashish came, spreading his arms in the air and shrugging his shoulders in frustration. He said something to them, and the three inmates of the White House went back to their white room!

The calls from the loud speakers continued, and the protest at the courtyard continued. Tension was high among both the prisoners and the police.

Asaf started a wave of complaints. "What? Are we going to sleep out tonight?"

The Cat answered sarcastically, "What is wrong with that? It has been a long time since we saw the moon and the stars."

Abu Haddid answered, trembling, "They will beat the crap out of us if we do not go in."

Comrade Imad felt the cloud of fear inside him vanish, and felt the jasmine bloom in his soul. He said loudly, "Guys, we will not go in until the Maghrib call to prayer." His voice was lost among the mingled voices and contradicting opinions.

Watwat, the trustee of the South Ward, said with a commanding voice, "Come on, let us go in, guys!"

Confusion spread in the courtyard and suggestions clashed; at this fluid time, the sit-down protest would have collapsed if it had not been for Shakeek's quick reaction. He held up Imad's hand with his right hand, Kurzum's hand with his left, and said, "We are sitting here; whoever wants to go in is welcome to do so."

Imad was happy and his heart was content, as if he were sitting on the grass at Yarmouk University, where he was when he was arrested. He remembered leading a protest in solidarity with the Al-Jaleel uprising in response to the Israeli government's confiscation of thousands of hectares of land from the Palestinians.

After that, things escalated. The three friends sat on the floor facing the gate, resting their backs against the edge of the water fountain. The movement of the prisoners around them was disturbed, and minutes later, Old Man came and sat down next to them. Then The Cat and Abu Zahra came and sat down. Most of the inmates sat down. Abu Haddid opened his mouth, which resembled a big hole complaining, panting like a thirsty dog. His large nostrils opened and closed nervously, but he did not sit down and did not go in.

Those who did not sit down continued to walk around the courtyard until the Maghrib call to prayer was heard. At that point, Comrade Imad, Shakeek, and Old Man rose and entered their wards without saying a word. The rest of the prisoners followed, and everyone breathed a sigh of relief!

Imad respected the support of Abu Laila Shakeek. He felt that he now knew him for who he really was.

Shakeek got his title from the mystery that surrounded his case. He was imprisoned for bouncing checks. Did he do it intentionally, trying to con someone, or was it bad luck? No one knew. His case was complex and hard to figure out. He was mysterious, and quiet. He never complained about anything, as if he had been born here. You never knew what he was thinking.

Imad remembered why he felt comfortable with the man as soon as he saw him. He looked just like the chemistry teacher that he had at his high school in Irbid. He was a cheerful guy; when he wanted to light a flame, he would ask the students for a light. He would say, "I know half of you smoke; I am sure one of you has a light." One of the students would quickly get a match out and light the wick.

In the wards, Shakeek never talked about himself, or about anyone else for that matter. He actually never spoke unless he had to. His voice was always tired and quiet. Perhaps these characteristics were what gained him the title Shakeek the Suspicious, as opposed to the many shady, suspicious characters that roamed the hallways of the prison. People sometimes deal with the things that they have a hard time understanding by giving obvious titles to classify them, or perhaps to help overcome their lack of ability to understand them.

Shakeek seemed in his fifties, very tall with a moderate weight. He had a black mustache and high forehead with curly hair and an olive complexion, and he always wore dark glasses. He was easygoing and rarely reacted to things. This mystery gave him a special status and placed him among the dignitaries of the prison. After the protest, Imad could see he looked younger, happier, and more enthusiastic; he seemed in his thirties.

■　■　■

Inside the wards, tension continued to mount. A long line formed in front of the urinals. No one started his Primus, no one talked to his neighbor, and no shopkeeper opened his little shop. Every ward had two shops: one for groceries, made of a small wooden box with a lock. The box contained a few cans of hummus and ful, sardines, tuna, condensed milk, biscuits, a packet of aspirin for headaches, and a can of Fem-Lax to help soften the stool. The other shop consisted of a large plastic bag, with smaller ones full of beads of different sizes and colors, threads, hooks, and needles of variable sizes. It also included tattoo supplies: ink, kohl, glue, a batch of thin and tall needles, and wax paper used to draw the art prior to tattooing it on the skin. Tattooing was a profitable profession in prison. Prayer beads, necklaces, and beaded cloths were a source of good income. The prisoners sold these products to the visitors and used them to bribe the guards and purchase spacious locations for their bedding.

After the Maghrib prayer, the guards counted the prisoners. The counting happened quietly. The prisoners started to calm down, and life slowly returned to normal. A quiet chatter started and then faded with the loud sound of Primuses lit everywhere, cooking food and boiling water for tea.

The inmates were soon dead asleep.

The Cage of the Righteous

After midnight, the police raided the wards, fully equipped with their batons and handcuffs. Imad was awake, trying to get rid of his worries by reading the second volume of *The History of Jobarti* when the lock on the ward's door rattled. He stood up and called to the ones around him. "Get up, they came for us."

Soon two guards pushed him to the ground, roughed him up, and twisted his arms behind his back. One of them blindfolded him while pushing his knee against Imad's chest. Imad could hardly breathe. Another guard cuffed him. He stopped feeling anything.

Imad woke up from his concussion, confused. He threw up and was aided by figures he was not able to recognize. He felt a little better after he threw up, and then heard The Cat laugh and say, "The dungeon is brighter with its guests."

Shakeek quietly asked, "How are you, Comrade?"

He answered, "Hungry."

Kurzum quickly added, "I am starving too."

The Cat stopped hopping around and said, "To hell with hunger." He then moved a stone inside the dungeon, stretched his hand into the dark space, and pulled out a container with a bunch of olives and a handful of dried bread. Then he ran to another corner, brought a bottle of water, and placed it in front of his guests. He sat down and handed the pieces of bread and the olives to his guests, as if he was Jesus in the painting of the Last Supper.

"Oh my God! I never tasted better olives in my life, or had a piece of bread more delicious than this!" said Imad.

"To health and prosperity," saluted Shakeek.

The Cat walked like a shadow puppet and started dancing and singing, "Turn me back into a child, and take my wealth away. Oh, Oh, Oh . . . Then I would have another chance to slowly grow up again."

His joy was contagious. They all got up, stood around The Cat, and started rhythmically clapping their hands while The Cat danced in the middle with agility and lightness.

They continued to sing old songs, and The Cat kept dancing. Their loud, joyous laughter was the type of laughter that lifted up the hard rocks of the low ceiling of the dungeon and caused the pure tears of the heart to flow.

Kurzum said, "May God protect us from the evil of laughter, and grant us His blessings."[34]

The Cat added, "And grant us something better than this."

Shakeek said, choking on his laughs, "They should have named you Canary, or Nightingale."

The Cat answered joyfully with a poetry line. "Gain pleasures from your today; nights rarely bring safety or play."

They spent the rest of the night laughing, chatting, and mocking their harsh life in prison.

They did not know what time of the day it was when the door of the dungeon opened and breakfast was served: a block of bread, a handful of olives, and three cups of tea. The Cat offered the food to his friends. They were his guests in this space where he was frequently placed.

They ate their food and fell asleep.

.   ■   ▪

When The Cat lightly kicked him to wake him up, he was dead asleep and not aware that he was in the dungeon. He turned over and continued to sleep.

The Cat whispered, "Wake up, Comrade, wake up."

"Oh, what Cat? You do not let anyone sleep!" He woke up, felt his stiff body, and tried to move his legs and arms.

"Wake up, Comrade, wake up. The floor of the dungeon is moist; it is not good to sleep on it for a long time. It is not good for your bones."

Imad looked around, surprised. His eyes blinked, trying to get accustomed to the darkness. He stood up to move his legs, bumped his head, and bent down to avoid the low and irregular ceiling of the dungeon.

"Come here by the door; the humidity is less here," said The Cat.

Imad sat next to The Cat by the entrance and rested his back against the thick wooden door.

"I want to tell you something."

Imad laughed. "What? Is Karma here?"

"I want to tell you something important, Comrade."

Imad laughed again. "What? Tell me."

"Do you see the stone that I was hiding the food behind?"

"All the stones look alike to me," said Imad.

"This is a small dungeon; its walls are blocked by symmetrical blocks!" The Cat added, laughing, "I checked them one by one. I had nothing to do. I was in no hurry. When the rocks were moved, guess what I found?" The Cat lowered his voice further and whispered, "I found a tunnel."

Imad asked, surprised, "Where does it lead to?"

"I crawled in, then I was afraid to suffocate, so I came back. First, I walked crouching, but when I reached deeper, I had to crawl."

"Are you thinking about running away, my friend?"

"I always think about running away."

Imad realized that was why he wanted to come back to the dungeon. Here he planned to look for a way out, day after day, until his plans were complete! Through this, he saw his freedom; he saw his village, the red poppies, the yellow chamomile flowers, and the mulberry trees! Imad felt a ray of light waking the scent of jasmine inside him and said, "Do you want me to run away with you?"

The Cat laughed and said, "Yes, right."

"Through the tunnel?"

"Through the gate."

"Which gate?"

"The main gate."

He felt that The Cat was taunting him. "Cat! Do not confuse me. You sneak out by the exterior gate to intentionally make them throw you in the dungeon?"

The Cat laughed and explained: "They will eventually get used to seeing me in the restricted area. They will keep putting me in the dungeon as a punishment, and when they get used to putting me there, they will stop paying attention to where I am."

"And when they stop paying attention?"

"On a cold, rainy day, I will slip through the gate to the street."

Imad thought, "Why is he telling me his plan?" Then he said to The Cat, "You puzzle me, Cat!" and continued thinking, "The Little Prince never gave explanations; he expected me to be like him, but unfortunately, I was unable to see the sheep in the box. I became like the old people; I myself have aged."

·   ·   ·

According to The Cat, and based on his experience in the dungeon, it was Maghrib. The door opened with a sharp, cracking sound that woke up the sleeping inmates inside. Lunch was brought in.

The Cat picked up the aluminum platter with rice and a few white broad beans and an old green plastic jug of water.

Kurzum took the jug, drank a little, gargled, stretched out his right hand, poured a little water, and wiped his face. Then Shakeek took the jug, put it down, turned south, and started getting ready to perform ablution. The Cat took the jug back! Shakeek raised his eyebrows in dismay.

The Cat said, "The water is not enough."

Kurzum asked, "Are we required to pray in these conditions?"

Without saying a word to either of them, Shakeek patted the walls with his hands, stirring some dust, and performed his ablution substituting dust for water. He then performed his Maghrib prayer combined with his Isha prayer.

This was the first time Imad ate prison food, but hunger can make you eat anything. They ate the rice, but each moved the few beans to the side, wanting to save them for the others to enjoy. Abu Laila Shakeek divided them equally among the friends, and the plate was cleaned.

After dinner, Kurzum and The Cat got up and walked in the space by the door beneath the highest part of the ceiling. With the ceiling so low in the other parts, it was hard for Imad and Shakeek to walk at the same time, so they sat in the corner, leaving space for their friends to move.

Every strong man in prison had his unique tattoo. Kurzum's tattoo was a snake. It was the only stretched out thing on his body. Everything else was square: his head was square, his face was square, and his nose was square. His body was strong like a wall. His light brown skin was covered with coarse hair. His mustache looked like a used toothbrush, and his lazy right eye gave him a devious look.

The Cat had bright eyes. His hair was long and straight. He trimmed his beard and mustache and regularly dyed his hair. Even though he was sixty, he looked younger than Kurzum, who was not more than thirty years old!

The Cat walked silently. Kurzum mumbled a few common curses and asked The Cat, "What are you thinking about? You're in a different mood today."

The Cat did not answer. He crossed his arms and sat cross-legged on the floor in front of Shakeek and said, "Entertain us, Abu Laila."

Shakeek smiled happily, perhaps because he was called by his real name, and said, "No one performs when you are around!"

The Cat cleared his throat and said to Kurzum, "Sit down, man; you are making us dizzy with your pacing."

Kurzum sat down and The Cat crossed his fingers, placed his arms on his knees, and started to tell a story. "Once upon a time, there was a city called Greece. The people in this city were shrewd and intelligent. There was nothing that they did not question and write about. Their god's name was Zeus, who bragged about their knowledge to the other gods. But the Greeks became arrogant and challenged Zeus. They said, 'Who is Zeus? We want to know him.' Zeus was angry. He went down to earth, dressed like them, and went to confront them. He met a young, arrogant man—your age, Comrade. He greeted him and asked, 'Is it correct that you know everything?'

"The young man answered pompously, 'Ask.'

"The god asked, "Do you know where Zeus is?'

"The young man looked up, looked down, and then stared at the god and said, 'I looked for him in the sky and didn't find him, and looked for him on earth and didn't find him. God is one of two: either me, or you.' Zeus was furious. He placed his hand under the city he loved, and turned it upside down. The city's buildings were destroyed, and the papers flew into the air and reached far places, where other people read them and learned from them. From that day on, all knowledge and understanding stemmed from the papers that the Greeks had written."

Imad said nothing. He was thinking, "Where did The Cat come up with this story? Is he an avid reader, or is it just a tale that gradually evolved as people told it, generation after generation, until it reached this dusty dungeon, in this form?"

Shakeek tucked his shoes under his head and stretched out his body. The rest of them did the same and went to sleep. Imad thought that this sinful group of people knew how to practice solidarity and advocacy and were able to stand their ground better than educated elites, frustrated politicians, and politicized Party members. Shakeek, for example, was calm by nature, but his actions proved that he was a man with courage and initiative.

Kurzum had been sentenced to seven years for armed robbery. He was cunning, careful, and anticipated things before they happened. On the other hand, The Cat was a petty thief. With a child's simplicity, he tore down all that restricted his free spirit.

These thoughts were disturbing to Imad's set of beliefs. He thought, "My logic was unable to dissect the present as it was. Distancing myself a little allowed me to see the elephant in the stomach of the snake and the sheep inside the box."

In the middle of the night, Imad felt the warmth of a body beside him. He woke up with Kurzum twisting and pushing his body next to him. He felt a silly embarrassment and turned toward Shakeek, who was sound asleep. There was no distance left between him and Kurzum. He held his breath; he could barely breathe. Was Kurzum intentionally touching him? Kurzum's back touched Imad's back, and he felt Kurzum's hand stretch past his waist, looking for . . . Is the man dreaming? Imad jumped up, yelling, "Kurzum!"

The Cat woke up. "What? What happened?"

Kurzum moved away and curled up and looked as if he was in deep sleep.

Without thinking, Imad yelled, "Dog!"

The Cat said nothing. He unrolled his shoes, gave one to Imad, and pointed to a place beside him.

Imad wrapped one of The Cat's shoes with his shirt, lay down, put his head on it, but couldn't go to sleep. He thought, "There are certain actions that are governed by the mind, which it rejects or understands; it accuses or excuses; it condemns or forgives. The body has to obey, and there are things that the body feels that the mind suppresses and pretends they are not there, or sails in a different direction, defying the mind and its logic. The body has its power, especially when it directs, wants, or desires. It has its temptations when it dances, or when it becomes joyous or elated. The body senses pleasures and yearns to be free and go wild. The mind, on the other hand, is the harness. Is the body made of a lowly clay and the mind of clear light? Is the body sin and the mind knowledge? The knowledge of the mind is soft and easy to scratch and forget, while the knowledge of the body is a tattoo mixed with desire, and hammered by the clamor of experience."

He continued to think: "For some strange reason, the body is punished for what the mind does! I could be whipped and thrown into prison for long, dark years for what I think. It is like a 'healer' that beats a 'possessed' body to ward off evil spirits. The body is kind and forgiving of the failings of the mind. It bears harm, sickness, deprivation, and prison; but in a blink of an eye it could withdraw from the game and leave us hanging in nothingness!"

Imad adjusted the shoe under his head and stretched out his body, staring into the transparent darkness. He missed his pillow and his bed. He even missed the whispering and chatter of the prisoners in the wards. It is incredible how quickly needs are reduced to basic ones. The dungeon dripped with the cold that the night brought, making the body think of the heat that keeps it warm. To be exact, the warmth of a close body—the warmth of Kurzum's body. Imad wondered, "Is Kurzum gay?" This was not known, despite the fact that this rumor haunted many of the inmates of all ages and trades. Imad heard about ways of bringing "newcomers" into these relationships. It started with being kind to the target, and allowing him, even encouraging him, to touch his behind until he gets erect. Then oral sex would be performed, and the target would be asked to return the favor. Gradually he joins the playing field!

He turned to his side, facing The Cat. Half his face was sunk into the shoe, and the other half was engulfed by the quietness of the night. The Cat's skinny body was stretched out a few centimeters away from his. He wished he could get closer. He watched him with affection; the pores of his body yearned to get closer. A crimson desire was awakened inside him. He wanted his warmth. His breath was filled with red desire, and in a moment of a blue flashing, he almost crawled toward The Cat. Instead, he turned to the other side facing the wall, licked the palm of his hand, blew off his venom, and went to sleep.

The sound of a fight woke him up!

Abu Laila Shakeek was choking Kurzum, slapping him and yelling, "You dirty lowlife!"

"He held me from behind; I swear I did not—"

"He held you?" Shakeek slapped him again. "You want to tarnish the reputation of the noblest man in prison, you lowlife?

Apparently, The Cat had told Shakeek. Imad tried to intervene and stop the fight.

"It is okay. Nothing happened, Abu Laila."

"Don't worry about it," said Abu Laila and slapped Kurzum again. "I know you are a filthy lowlife."

Kurzum escaped the grip of Shakeek, turned his face to the side, and said, "I know who beat the manager who was caught . . ."

Shakeek's face turned blue. His jaw chattered with anger, and he raised his hand, determined to finish Kurzum, but the door suddenly opened, and Abu Laila's fist stayed up in the air.

The guard did not bring them breakfast. Instead, he said, "Come out, all of you."

A Coup

They were out! Even though they had been gone for only two nights, many things had changed!

Their demands were met, and the prisoners were allowed to stay out until the Maghrib prayer call!

A big blue rectangular sign with fancy script replaced the black sign with plain text, Irbid Prison, on the front gate. The fancy new sign said, "The Hashemite Kingdom of Jordan/National Security Agency/The Directorate of Rehabilitation and Reform/Irbid Center for Rehabilitation and Reform."

Old Man commented, "What does this mean? Are we retarded? If they are ashamed of the word prison, why don't they call it 'Aunt's House'? Isn't that what people say when they don't want to mention the word 'prison'? Don't they say, 'He went to his aunt's house'?"

New inmates arrived and others were released. A big, strong inmate called Abu al-Ganani—the father of bottles—joined them. His reputation preceded him. Shakeek was released suddenly without satisfying the curiosity of anyone about the cause of his imprisonment or sudden release. Haj Mulqi was sent to retirement. He was replaced by Officer 'Attalah Baik! Sergeant Hayder was promoted to deputy, transferred to the Traffic Directorate, and replaced by Sergeant Younis, who was put in charge of the interior gate of the prison!

Masses became the trustee at the East Ward in place of Watoot, and Asaf was moved and put in charge of the North Ward, replacing Kurzum. Abu Haddid remained in charge of his golden Ward in the South!

Kurzum was whipped in the middle of the courtyard because he was heard saying, "The deer was replaced by monkeys."

Further, a decision was made to transfer the Comrade from the North Ward to the White House! The Comrade did not like his new residence. He felt as if he had been exiled to a desolate island. He walked up the two light wooden steps covered with a tin roof leading the new room. The entrance door was painted white to separate it from the other black doors of the prison. What a luxury!

The distinguished inmates of his new residence were not pleased with his presence. They ignored him and continued watching the small television, one of their privileges, placed on a shelf next to the door. He spread out his bedding, ignored them too, and pretended to be busy by flipping the pages of Arar's[35] book *The Veiled Bedouin*, without reading a word.

Hiss, hiss, hiss . . . The broadcasting stopped.

During the technical difficulty, Hashish, the man in charge of the room, squinted and asked Imad, "What? Do you now support the government?"

Imad took his eyes off the book and asked sarcastically, "Which government?"

"Ha, ha, ha . . . ," the man laughed and added, "The government that sentenced you for ten years."

The rest of the residence laughed.

Ala al-Din Marlboro coughed a little to clear his throat and catch the attention of the audience and said sarcastically, "Do you understand politics?"

Imad said seriously, "Why? What about the topic interests you?"

Marlboro was taken aback; his eyes rolled in their sockets in confusion, and he stuttered, "Politics, I mean politics; aren't you a political prisoner?"

Abu Zaki Canary noted, "In the Canary Islands, no one cares about politics—there are wine, women, and lots of money; no politics there."

Hassan Transistor volunteered to pick up where the discussion stopped. He pushed his glasses back and said, "What do you think about the Geneva Convention?"

Imad answered with the alertness of an attentive student. "Palestine will be freed by resistance and not conferences."

His Excellency commented, moving his pink cheeks: "By God, good."

They laughed to please His Excellency.

Abu Jamil the Engineer, or the Pipe as he was called here, was a graduate of Red Moscow. It had been told that he was a radical Communist there, but now he denied that and dismissed it. Touching his silver hair, he said sarcastically, "Now the great Soviet Union, ha, ha, supports a new Geneva Convention."

Imad quickly answered, "Why should I care?" and immediately regretted it. He felt ashamed, as if he was responsible for the Soviet Union's failed foreign policy.

Abu Zaki Canary stretched his arms toward his television, which was still displaying the interrupted signal, and said, "How long do we have to wait? Come on, boy, get up and change the channel to Syrian."

Tuj got up, looking for the Syrian station under a flood of directions from the audience.

Imad felt an unexplained discomfort. He did not want to be at the bottom of the pack here. He was not exactly the last. There were six of them, and the seventh was their servant. He fell somewhere between the sixth and the servant—Tuj, who lived by the entrance of the room.

■   ■   ■

Every place has its own scent. The cells smelled of urine, blood, and flesh; the prison, vomit and DDT;[36] the wards, fart and fried onion; the dungeon, moist dust and the stench of mildew; and the White House, tobacco and the smell of burning animal fat.

The room was square with a wooden roof. It had a window facing east and a wall closet in the south side of the room. It had its own small courtyard with a bathroom, a sink, and a faucet. Next to it sat a basil plant and a velvet coleus. At the other side stood a large clay jar filled with water, and rocks arranged to facilitate cooking. Perhaps because of these additions, it was called the White House.

Imad's first night in the new place was sleepless.

When he was still at the Detention Center, they called his father to see him, and they said to his father, "Your son is a Communist and an infidel."

His father answered, "An infidel—this is for God to decide. A Communist—this is politics, between you and him. But I will break the hand that touches my son."

After the visit, they stopped "suspending" him. Actually, they stopped the physical torture altogether!

"Does tribal influence make life inside prison easier?

"Are they trying to isolate me from other prisoners?"

In his dream, he saw the inmates of the White House turned to security agents sitting around a large table discussing his case, and he was in the middle of all of that, lost. He woke up with a dry mouth and went to the courtyard to drink some water; the room's door was open. He could see the moonlight. The moon agitated his fears; he tried to escape his thoughts by staring at the details of the empty courtyard.

To the north was the kitchen window, and next to it was the juvenile delinquent ward, and next to it, the East Ward, for smugglers. It was the largest and most modern among all the rooms. It was built in the late seventies after Jordan's bloody war with the PLO.

The northern part of the prison consisted of bathrooms, sinks, washrooms, and the dungeon, with an emergency exit on the top, always kept closed.

He leaned on his pillow, thinking, "Did Sinan Pasha know when he designed Ottoman buildings, castles, and horse stables that they would one day be converted to misery chambers?"

He held his pillow tight and said to himself, "In the morning, I will ask the administration to return me to my place at the South Ward; otherwise . . . otherwise, I will recant . . . and be done."

The Cobia Pen

It was dawn, the special time that stirs the soul.

The juveniles came out with their long brooms and plastic buckets, washed the courtyard, and quickly disappeared. Dawn, a perfect time for silence, what a glorious moment! He loved dawn. It was his special time at this small spot on Earth. He wished that they would take their time opening the doors of the wards so that he could enjoy more of the early quietness.

The sun rose. Its golden rays peeked through an opening in the window and filled his heart with glad tidings. He watched the particles of dust dancing in the golden rays and followed them through the window. He listened to the clamor of the bustling city rise and smelled the fumes from the cars climbing the hill next to the prison. He looked at the sun and pleaded, "Free me, O glorious sun, from the follies of the White House. Nothing else could take me away from the watching eyes of the guards. Let me climb your streaming rays into your wide horizons, to freedom."

The sun ended its brief visit to his window, pulling away its last golden rays. Movement filled the prison's courtyard. He went out to Tamouni's Café.

"Best coffee cup for the Effendi."

"I don't want coffee, Tamouni, I want tea."

"The Effendi!" He did not like the new title and was eager for the time to pass so that he could rid himself of it. He asked Younis to arrange a meeting with the new warden.

Tamouni handed him a fresh, hot cup of tea. He drank it slowly, imitating the way the *Zogrut* drank their tea. He took long, slow sips, complained, and followed each sip with a deep breath. His performance went unnoticed. It did not bring him close to them again. He got up and walked around. An "effendi," estranged from the prisoners he left, and rejected by the prisoners he joined!

Atalla Baik called him. The Baik was a miserable officer with a round head, thin hair, stubby nose, small mouth, and plain eyes. His features were lost on his massive, dark face. His face definitely looked like the bottom of a semicircular skillet used for baking bread on an open fire.

The Baik said, in an intimidating manner, "We moved you to the White House to bring you back to your senses."

Imad felt the confession paper folded in his pocket and said, "But I was fine in the South Ward."

As if he hadn't heard a word of what Imad said, the new Warden went on rambling about his new goals for the prison, and discussing his innovative approach aligned with reform and rehabilitation. He explained, "Prisoners are equal in my eyes, like the "teeth of a comb."[37] No one is big except our King. I am not going to tolerate strikes, protests, sit-downs, or troubles. Mercy will be scarce, and discipline will rule." He was indirectly referring to the management style of the former warden. He added, "The time for a strike here and a strike there is over. It is gone with the Haj, God bless him. The old times are over, gone!"

"I want to go back to my old ward."

"Ha, ha, ha. Don't even think about that." He frowned and raised his voice. "Choose one of two: the White House or the dungeon?"

Imad answered with no hesitation. "The dungeon."

The Baik's stare was in true Jordanian style. He made it as harsh as he could muster, and yelled, "No! My decision is not subject to change."

He rang the bell. A frightened guard appeared, saluted, and stood erect.

Atalla said, "Cuff him and return him to the White House!"

■   ■   ■

He spent the second night in the White House handcuffed. His pillow was softer that night, and the jasmine bush stretched into his soul, vibrant and green. He fell into a deep, comfortable sleep. He said to himself, "Comrade, no one will believe that you could come back from the interrogation chamber to your cell bloody and happy, except those who have lived through the experience. No one will recognize your joy in having your hands cuffed, except your pillow!"

He wondered, "Am I insane?!"

In the morning, the prisoners came out to see the "handcuffed" inmate of the White House.

The Comrade went out and sat in the exterior courtyard across from the large water jar. Abu Zahra came holding the chess box, which he went nowhere without, under his arm; he greeted Imad and started crying . . .

Asaf was very angry. "Sons of bitches." He threatened to "report" them to the Pasha.

Watoot, the deposed trustee of the East Ward, held his arm tight and said, encouragingly, "Don't worry—a crisis and it will pass."

Kurzum twisted his lower lip angrily and said, threatening the Warden, "No problem. More to come . . ."

Old Man sat beside him, working tirelessly on putting the final touches on a beaded necklace he was working on, and said, "They moved you so that you can get used to it. Stay brave." He then handed him the finished necklace. "A gift from me."

It was an incredible necklace, woven with soft colored beads, arranged according to the colors of the rainbow. Beautiful and meticulously woven.

Imad said, "But . . ." He did not say what he thought: "What do I need it for? Who would I give it to . . . ?"

"The gift can't be returned, Comrade."

He inspected the necklace admiringly to please Old Man and thanked him. Imad liked Old Man.

Old Man was serving a life sentence. He had already finished ten years and had ten years left. He said that he had to kill a man! This "urgency" seemed more convincing to Imad today than it had at any other time.

At noon, The Cat ditched his work and came to see his friend.

The difference between the respectable residence of the White House and the kid with handcuffs presented an irony that made The Cat laugh. He fell on the ground and whispered, "This man is crazy." He then moved closer to Imad and said, "Abu Haddid said, 'The Comrade sold us out,' but Old Man shut him up." Then he changed his voice, imitating Old Man, and said, "Fear God, man!"

The Cat continued, "Kurzum commented on your move to the White House, saying that some people get everything, and others get nothing!"

Imad laughed and said, "Let us stop gossiping!"

The Cat said, "Can I light a cigarette for you?"

"No."

The Cat whispered, "I brought you a handful of jasmine."

"You also like jasmine!"

"I am scared of its fragrance. I am not used to it. I like poppy."

"Poppy?"

"Yes; it is one color, red or red. It is bright and humble; it grows everywhere, in the meadows, on the mountains, in the neighborhoods, on the hedges. If you pick it, it withers, and if you leave it, it grows more. Have you ever seen anyone planting poppies or selling poppies? Have you ever seen poppies detained in a room, or tied in a bundle? Poppies are free!"

Imad laughed. "A Cat and a philosopher!"

The Cat replied, joyfully, "A Cat and a thief, a Cat and a plumber, a Cat and a comedian, a Cat and . . ."

Marlboro added sarcastically, "A Cat and a bird . . ."

The Cat laughed and said, "I wish to become a bird and fly."

Tuj interrupted, "He means a snitch, that kind of bird, ha, ha, ha . . ."

The Cat felt stabbed. He pulled himself up slowly and sat next to Imad, as if an arrow had pierced his chest.

Imad threw his arms around The Cat and said nothing. Then he told The Cat, "Yesterday, I was lying down watching a spider dangling from a thread in its web, descending to the corner. I wished I could turn into a spider for one hour. No, one hour is not enough; a day is sufficient to climb the wall and cross the barbed wires at the top of the fence. I will stroll by the guard's hut and stick my sticky tongue at him in mockery, and walk to the other side."

He was silent for a moment, and then asked, "How fast can a spider go, walking?" Without waiting for an answer he continued, "There, at the edge of the wall by the Warden's window, I will intentionally hang on my fragile thread and watch them panic about my escape, then keep on going down."

He added, "How long would it take a spider to repel ten meters down, with one more minute spying at the Warden's office?

"Now, I will cross the road . . .

"What if I was squashed by someone walking down the street, or flattened by the tires of a speeding car?

"I should wait until it is dark, when the traffic stops, before I cross.

"No. No. This is not a solid plan. What if I stayed a spider forever?

"What kind of life do spiders live? What do they do? How do they weave their web and catch their prey?

"Even if I succeeded, do I want to spend my life catching bugs?

"The life of the spider is not fun. I prefer to become a bird, flap my wings and fly. That is better.

"I will land on the barbed wire over the fence; look at the walls for the last time, barbed wires, guns, sleeping quarters, cells, the dungeon, and the kitchen with its repulsive stench . . .

"I would bend my neck a little and tilt my head, like birds do, and say goodbye to the people at the courtyard, then fly away.

"I would flap my wings over the walls, pass by the guard standing ready by his machine gun at the tall observation tower, and fly away, sailing in the wide blue sky, forever."

The Cat laughed and said, "A beautiful story! It reminds me of Kafka's cockroach, Comrade!"

Imad opened his mouth wide. "The Cat, an educated deviant or talented thief?" He quickly added, "How do you know about Kafka! Do you read? I mean read books. I mean you are . . . ?"

"I am a Cat, ha, ha, I was born a Cat."

■   ■   ■

Warden Atalla's hasty decision made the prisoners sympathetic with the Comrade and annoyed the residents of the White House.

Nazmi Hashish was a high-ranking officer in the Narcotic Investigation Directorate. His sentence was "Losing government property worth thousands of dinars through arson." Here, he loved to smoke his hookah in the evenings while taking his walk followed by his servant Tuj, who walked behind him carrying the hookah's water infused with bay leaves, bubbling. Hashish blew the smoke of his pipe with the arrogance of a general. He covered his bald head with a keffiyeh and iqal, wore a white thobe concealing his oval-shaped belly, and carried fancy blue prayer beads worthy of his status. He constantly bragged about the "good old days" when he was on the force, and compared them to the miserable condition of today's police. The subject of his criticism today was the Comrade. "Why would they dignify someone who has no loyalty or patriotism by placing him in the White House?!"

Hassan Transistor worked at the Internal Revenue Department. His size was transistor, his shape was transistor, his glasses were transistor, and the silver cross on his chest was transistor; everything except his thick, wide, blond mustache was small. He called himself a Baathist, for the mere fact that he went to college in Iraq. This also made him interested in public affairs; he was always listening to a transistor radio that he usually placed very close to his ear. He considered his position towards the Comrade ideological and not personal.

Imad asked him, "You were a college graduate, on your way up, and have not had a chance to live your life yet. What made you get mixed up with bribery?"

"Brother, I really didn't mean it. It was not my intention. I was not even thinking about it. I once went with one of the old-timers in the agency to estimate income tax for a big merchant. When we were leaving, he said, 'Give me your car key.' I said, 'I have no car.' He then said, 'Give me your house address.' I gave it to him. I thought that he was going to send me a radio, an iron, a television at best. When I went home and the package arrived, it was 5,000 dinars! I was elated . . . I bought a car, a television, a refrigerator, and I had a little more left. From that day on, I started asking for it myself."

Marlboro interrupted, "Tell us how you got a job with the Internal Revenue Department. As far as I am aware, the Baathists are like Communists and Liberationists: they don't get hired, and their passports are held up . . ."

He said nothing, but Marlboro pressed. "Unless you started working for them!"

Hassan pushed the tip of his glasses back with his fingers and started saying something, then swallowed what he wanted to say and remained silent.

There was also a former Communist, engineer Abu Jamil, the Pipe. He was in his fifties, tall, skinny, bold, with a head like a shiny aluminum cylinder. He shaved his beard and mustache, trying to look younger. Does he look like a pipe? Perhaps. He was accused of embezzlement, working with a private company that supplies pipes to the Water Authority. His story was, "Man, they were short a few pipes, so they sent us to prison!" The Engineer cared about "prestige," trying to gain brownie points with His Excellency. He looked at Imad and said, "It is getting ridiculous; they are now bringing us trash!"

Meanwhile, the former customs officer, Marlboro's (it was obvious why they called him Marlboro) most distinguished feature was his stretched face, as if he was blowing on something. Above his protruding mouth sat a long, pointed nose, and under it a pointed beard, and under it a large Adam's apple that looked like it was jumping out of his long, skinny neck. He truly looked like an upside-down letter M on the Marlboro package! His complaint was, "There is no place here, Abu Nazmi. It is a small room, four by five meters! They are turning it into a common ward!"

There was another man, in his forties, always freshly showered. He was in charge of the bath. Despite his cleanliness, he was not well dressed: a checkered jacket over a wrinkled thobe or slacks, a shirt and a tie without a jacket, a zipped sweater over khaki pants! His perfectly bald head on the top looked just like a hat; his goatee connected to his mustache formed another circular shape. He was always smiling like a realtor. He actually worked as a realtor—and still does—he sold land that he did not own in West Amman, went to spend the money he made vacationing in the Canary Islands, and returned to do time in prison. He made the calculation ahead of time, accepted the ramifications, and was now contentedly serving his sentence. He fully deserved his title: Abu Zaki Canary. He was credited with being the first to bring a television to prison. He looked at the Comrade and said, laughing, "Ha, ha, perhaps you have no television in your house; watch here, courtesy of the generous ones!"

His Excellency was one of the "sloths." This title was not actually used in his presence. He went to jail for issuing a fake ID! He constantly stared at the celling, poking his plump, moist lips—which looked like two halves of a ripe fig—together to blow perfectly round circles of smoke from his Kent cigarette. His excuse was, "I thought I was rendering a service to His Majesty, but it turned out to be the mistake of a lifetime!" He never explained what the mistake was or how it was counted against him. He relaxed his round pink face and continued to blow his smoke circles. It was beyond him to openly express his disapproval of the presence of the Comrade.

Despite all that had been said earlier, or perhaps because of it, the residents of the White House did everything they could to pressure the Warden, who finally gave the orders to take off the Comrade's handcuffs.

Imad sat on his bed, taking his mind off the people in the room, with their antagonism and gloomy faces, by drawing the familiar faces of his friends. Abu Haddid was spontaneous but held grudges. He was like a wolf; if you pushed him, he would create a ruckus. The Cat, a free spirit that found himself in a cage. A cat that thought it was a singing bird in a wide horizon! Old Man was wise, patient, and calm—like a camel, when angered he became hard to handle. Asaf was smooth and slippery; when you thought you had him in your grasp, he slipped away to the other side—his fangs ready, like a snake. Kurzum was a fox, waiting; he hit and quickly hid, capable of adapting to his environment. Abu Zahra was weak, frightened, like a lizard, scared of every moving thing.

Imad stopped drawing and wondered, "Who am I? I wish I knew!"

The White House

The crescent indicating the start of the month of fasting was sighted. Imad slowly became one of the "furniture owners" in prison. He replaced his prison-issued mattress with a wool one that his mother brought from home. He thought, "How sweet is the scent of a mother infused in the freshly washed linen."

He choked with tears. "I love you, Mother; my tears fall yearning for your warmth. Forgive me, Mother. Only you see in my faults suspended signs of loyalty, and see in my shortcomings, perfection; and continue to mention my name when you supplicate, praying at dawn."

He also owned a shelf on which he placed his books. He treated himself by creating a lamp made of a cardboard cylinder with a bulb and hung it by his bed. The light from the lamp allowed him to read when the masters slept. He wrote on it in English with a broad font "Konnash Bulb."

A relationship developed between his pen and pillow. What he wrote with his pen he discussed with his pillow, and what the pillow whispered, he jumped and recorded with his pen.

Long presence generates intimacy. With time, the White House became accustomed to his presence. This allowed him to intervene in the endless disputes and shifting loyalties among its "elite" residents.

The prisoners became accustomed to the unwelcome interference of the new warden and welcomed the holy month that broke the monotony of their daily routines. Imad was enamored with the sunrays that came through the window and landed on his pillow every morning. He enjoyed the noise coming from the loudspeakers in the morning, announcing the start of the day, mixed with the sounds generated by the inmates going about their daily lives. It pleased him that the prison noise masked the noise of the cars climbing the nearby hill.

He became used to the smell of tobacco from the Engineer's pipe, the smoke circles His Excellency blew into the air, the cough of Hashish smoking his hookah, the clatter of Mr. Marlboro's prayer beads smacking into each other, and the ill humor of Tuj, the servant. He started listening to Radio Monte Carlo broadcasted in Arabic with Hassan Transistor, and spent time alone listening to Fairuz's songs in the mornings and Umm Kulthum in the evenings. When alone, his tears flowed freely without him knowing why he cried, but he seemed to find pleasure in doing so.

In the morning, he read the daily papers in the company of His Excellency, and at night, he watched television as a favor from Abu Zaki Canary.

■　　■　　■

Ramadan crescent disappeared. It was mid-September; the nights were laced with tender coolness. Waiting for the sighting of the new crescent announcing the start of Eid al-Fitr, he flipped the pages of *Evenings at Wadi Al-Yabes*, by the renowned Jordanian poet Arar, and read one of his poems that was very famous among patriotic Jordanians. They took pride in claiming it to be the first "rhythmic free verse" written in modern Arabic poetry.

> The crescent appeared, and we saw its shadow.
> Then, the jailer came, and shut the window.
> Evening arrived, wrapped us in echoes.
> Greeted us with gloominess, spreading through the meadow.
> Silence shattered, when chains yawned and woke up the fellow.

Apparently, the important thing is not to just read, but to read again and understand.

Imad imagined Arar, in his prison cell, pouring his soul into his poems, on the night of Eid al-Fitr, writing with his left hand from the right to the left. He imagined Arar left-handed, even though no one ever said that about him.

A distant sound from a gramophone with Umm Kulthum's voice reached him:

The chant of soul touches the souls
The heart knew him when he came
I called on him, but he flew with no wings.
His cries tore open the chest of time.

Was the voice coming from an old gramophone from Arar's time, or from a transistor radio carried by a bored guard?

"I am on the hilltop of Irbid, a prisoner, and Arar, who was in prison here fifty years ago, on the foot of the hill, buried."

He tried drawing Arar's portrait: black, sharp eyes, in his early twenties, carefree, simply dressed, and void of any type of pretense. He looked at the portrait unsatisfied, and drowned himself in a wave of dark depression that frequently attacked him like all other prisoners, sometimes for a reason, and many times for no reason at all. He cried without knowing why, then reached out to the pants hanging on a nail over his head, searched his pockets, took out the "recanting" statement, and read it.

"Denounce!" Arab radio stations were full with indignation and condemnation statements.

"Pledge loyalty!" He never thought of or heard any Comrade object to a king or a government. The Party's platform was "towards a liberalized national governance."

"To the wise government." Each administration, even the prison administration, claimed to be wiser than its predecessors were.

"Denounce, pledge loyalty, the wise government—all are words without meaning!

"There is a fine line between calling a confession boldness and thirst for freedom, or considering it meekness, a failure, and vulnerability.

"I am the one who decides, not the Party, not the Intelligence apparatus, not my friends, and not my opponents. What is all the fuss about? I should go ahead, denounce, declare loyalty, and pronounce the government wise!"

When he decided that, he saw himself like an animal in a circus who leaves the fenced camp to enter a small, heavy cage that stays with him wherever he goes!

He put the paper away with the other papers and spent the rest of the night tossing, turning, and trying to decide.

"Hand it in to them? Don't hand it in?

"Give up? Don't give up?"

The Narrator

I am the narrator, Hashem Gharaibeh. I was going through old prison papers, which I wrote thirty-three years ago. Suddenly, a dried jasmine flew from between the papers like a butterfly the color of hay and landed in my hand, connecting my soul to the scent of jasmine mixed with the pride of youth, the age of inspiration, the warmth of dreams, and the sanctity of personal dignity. The ink on the paper glowed, awakening the memories sleeping in the palm of time.

I recall that "Imad" learned about the Party a year and a half prior to his arrest, during his effort to establish a student union. He found among its members educated people that he could talk to about structuralism, existentialism, and the definition of Communism, and argue ways to establish Arab unity. He met activists who filled his dreams with the ideas of freedom, liberty, and social justice. He followed "Abu Musa" and truly understood what it meant to be a member of an organized political party.

Was this what sustained him in facing "prison?" Was it the warmth of belonging to a special, intimate group, or the thrill of being different and unique?

Thoughts were clouding his mind! The brightness generated from his effort to understand was what led him to insist on saying "no." This was the secret that bound his fellow students together and led them to protest for the sake of, or in defense of something. It was the same concept that attracted the inmates to him in prison in mutual admiration!

What was the elusive, mysterious thing that he was afraid to lose?! That radiance that comes from self-respect and the sweet belief in one's ideas, which shines through the eyes when one argues about something he is convinced about.

What guarded him from the consequences of "recanting"? Was it daring to have power, even if it was just the power of having the right to say "no"?

What was courage?

He looked at a paper on which he had written, "What do I have left if I am robbed of the right to say 'no'?"

Freedom was to have the right to say "no."

"No" was strong, and full of possibilities, and "yes" was easy, meek, and barren.

"No" was the key to freedom. Nothing makes people dare to act like the breeze of freedom.

Eid

When the call to Fajr prayer sounded, a breeze loaded with the scent of jasmine took him by surprise. He felt refreshed, moved his papers away, got up, and went to drink a cup of water from the clay jug outside the room. On this dawn of September, Eid al-Fitr, the first Thursday of Shawwal 1397, corresponding with 15 September 1977, he was swept with a unique sense of tenderness. Sitting in the small courtyard in front of the White House, ignoring the morning cold, he watched the breaking of dawn with great appetite. The sounds of the melodies of Eid that flooded the city's sky filled him with tremendous joy.

Allah'u'Akbar, Allah'u'Akbar, Praised be God.
Allah'u'Akbar, Allah'u'Akbar, No God but God.

He could see his mother's face between the jasmine flowers, sweeping the entrance of the house in the white morning light.

He could hear the whooshing water; "Was my father up performing his ablution?"

He could smell the freshly baked bread; "Were those the Eid loaves my mother bakes?"

The distance, whooshing water, the aroma of roasted coffee, the smell of freshly baked bread, and the scent of jasmine were in the house, in the village, in the city!

Was there a city, a village, a house?

Was there jasmine, bread, coffee, and water?

Did Eid arrive?!

Prison does not consume people; it consumes the taste of things and their scents.

■   ■   ■

During Eid, certain visitors were expected.

Imad was happy that a number of his friends from the university dared to come visit. They did not talk about politics and university affairs. They chatted about girls, university daily life, and normal routines. One of them slipped a paper into the sleeve of the Comrade!

Next to them was the Engineer, bending to talk to his wife and daughter, who had attracted the attention of the young men with her commanding presence and red, wavy hair. One of his friends said, "I know this girl; I have seen her at the university."

Imad noticed that her father had asked one of the boys who served at the window to bring some water; the boys brought them water from Tamouni's Café. She placed the aluminum cup at the ledge of the window separating the visitors from the prisoners and did not drink! The Comrade excused himself from his friends for a minute and went in, brought a clean water pitcher and a few paper cups, and poured water for the Engineer, his wife, and his daughter, of course. Then he went around pouring water for those who asked among the rest of the visitors. The Engineer commented, showing off his expertise, "This water is from Rahoub well. There is no purer source in Jordan. The water tower on the hill is the only water tower in Irbid connected to it. The rest get their water from al-Zarqa oasis."

His friends left the visitors' screen, and he went on picking up the used paper cups in an empty bag. The girl handed him one and said, "You are?"

The Engineer gave in to his daughter's interest in the Comrade and invited him to talk to her by introducing her. "My daughter Maha started college this year; she heard about you from her friends."

The pampered, pretty princess wanted to meet the bad boy that the other students had talked about with panic and respect! The Engineer was proud of his daughter; she was studying English literature at Yarmouk University. Imad was happy to meet the bronzed girl with the smart hazel eyes.

Humoring her, he said, "There is no doubt that His Honor the Engineer will come out innocent."

She moved her bangs to the side and said, "Really!"

Through the whole visit, he had not heard her say a complete sentence; despite that, her short phrases fluttered around him like colored butterflies.

He walked alone in the prison courtyard. "Oh, how beautiful it is to be inspired!"

Hassan Transistor passed by. "Good evening, Comrade." The Comrade was not interested in speaking to anyone.

He wanted to enjoy the celebrating evening with its heavenly sky, alone. He recalled the face of the redheaded girl, her hazel smiling eyes, and her proud nose surrounded by freckles. He enjoyed watching with her the clouds changing shapes, journeying towards the east on their way to the crimson meadow where he had spent his early childhood. Thinking of his childhood brought a smile to his face. "Why do we remember our childhood in the presence of who . . ." He hesitated a little . . . "in the presence of whom we love?"

The birds sang on their way to their nests above the tall wall. Only The Cat knew how to catch him in his private moment. He walked beside him without saying a word, and when the whistle of the guards sounded, calling the prisoners to their wards, he seized the moment and asked, smiling, "Did you like her?"

The comment surprised Imad. He opened the palm of his hand in gesture and said smiling, "You're a fox!"

The Cat slapped Imad's open hand hard; the folded paper in Imad's sleeve fell down. He picked it up quickly and walked back to his bed at the White House.

At night, he tried to get close to the Engineer; he asked him about the status of his case—was there going to be a trial soon? The man was busy filling his pipe and watching *Peyton Place* on television.

Hassan Transistor was interested in predicting the development of events in soap operas, soccer games, or films they watched on television, but he rarely guessed right. This made him the focus of the White House residents' sarcasm. Tonight he was right, for a change. The movie was about a pretty woman married to a rich old man, but in love with her driver. The debate about the film generated more interest between the prisoners than even the local soccer games that were the subject of constant predictions and debates. The Engineer and Hassan took the side of the wife; Marlboro and Canary sided with Nazmi Hashish, supporting the rich husband; and His Excellency remained neutral.

The Engineer got out of his way and asked Imad, "The Comrade with the wife, of course?"

Imad laughed and said, "I am with the driver."

Canary commented sarcastically, "Of course—a Communist, friend of blade cutters and hookers."

"True."

The audience was divided into two equal camps, three against three.

Imad was happy to be on the side of the Engineer for other, romantic reasons.

Having the Comrade on the other side annoyed Abu Nazmi and made him eager to get the Minister to take sides. "Your Excellency, you would not tolerate cheating, would you?"

His Excellency put out his Kent cigarette without finishing it, coughed a little, and said nothing.

His Excellency's indifference annoyed Hashish; he commented, "Sloths have no chivalry."

His Excellency pretended not to hear him and continued to listen with little interest. The only thing that indicated his presence was his occasional short coughs.

When the old man ran after his wife with a rifle in his hand, Hashish rubbed his small beard with excitement and yelled, "Kill her, the cheater!"

Tuj was perplexed! His feelings were with the Engineer's team, but he could not muster the courage of going against Abu Nazmi. His Excellency continued his indifference and random, unexplained coughs. This angered Abu Nazmi, who went on cursing the wife, the driver, and lazy people—ready to curse whoever did not take his side.

Something inside al-Tuj snapped; he suddenly lost his temper and threw his sock at the Minister, yelling, "Why are you so high and mighty and silent? If you don't like what we say, enlighten us with your views."

The Minister's face turned red. He sat up, straightened his posture, and stared at the servant!

Tuj realized his mistake, but instead of retreating, he raised his voice higher and said, "Are you waiting for the Prime Minister to step down and say to you, come take my place? To hell with you!"

The Minister's eyes bulged with disbelief, and unexpectedly, he picked up the ashtray and threw it at Tuj. It missed him and hit the door. The half-smoked cigarettes flew everywhere.

Even though Tuj felt that the Minister had gone too far, he bent and picked up the cigarette butts, mumbling, "It's too late for you; let go and put it to rest."

The atmosphere became tense. All stopped talking. The place was charged with the hissing of silence loaded with pent-up feelings and thoughts.

Tuj crawled to his bed by the entrance. Hashish held his lips tight, concealing his laugh. But Canary could not hold it in anymore and burst out laughing. The Minister's face turned redder.

Imad went to his bed in a good mood, took advantage of the tense atmosphere in the room, turned his lamp on, opened his notebook, dropped in it the paper that was in his sleeve, opened it, and read:

THE JORDANIAN COMMUNIST PARTY—THE POLITICAL UNIT
Private: A Special Report to Advanced Cadres in the Party

The Party observed from current American politics that President Carter supports the comprehensive approach to the Middle East problems, specifically a homeland for Palestinians in the West Bank and Gaza Strip with links to Jordan. He also supports the holding of the Geneva Convention again with the participation of the Soviet Union and all parties involved in the conflict.

Menachem Begin on the other hand, denies that the Palestinians have any national rights, and sees that Security Council Resolution 242 does not apply to the West Bank and the Gaza Strip. He opposes the convening of an international conference with the participation of the Soviet Union. The Zionist lobby in America is active in its effort to block Carter's plans to convene an International Conference. There is a problem with the Arab position as well. While Jordan and Syria favor a unified representation of the Arab delegation that supports the Geneva Convention, in the event it is convened, Egypt's Sadat prefers sending separate delegations.

Winning the election by the right wing Government in Israel headed by Menachem Begin last May put an end to three decades of control of the Labor

Party over the successive Israeli Governments. It also resulted in the arrival of Likud to power in Israel, which is expected to result in a major change in Israel foreign policy. The pragmatic Labor was preoccupied with Israel's security; meanwhile, Likud is a nationalist party that strongly advocates "Israel Homeland" and rejects any claims by Jordan relating to Jordanian sovereignty in the West Bank, and rejects any right of Palestinians to self-determination. The new Israeli Government will not only keep the West Bank, it will continue to carry out its policies to move Palestinians from the West Bank to the East Bank. In addition, the new Prime Minister Menachem Begin was a leader of a right-wing terrorist group and a member of The National Unity Government headed by Levi Eshkol. He previously proclaimed that Palestine is located east of the Jordan River, and the only thing that needs to change is the monarchy because the majority of the population in Jordan are Palestinians!

Accordingly, resuming negotiations regarding the West Bank is unlikely based on the positions of both Israel and Jordan.

"The Jordanian Option" is buried, and replaced by the "Egyptian Option"

September 1977

Imad smiled after reading the report. "Not worth a kilo of cucumbers! Who am I supposed to talk to about the content of this report?"

He took out the beaded necklace Old Man had given him, discretely checked it out, and thought, "Should I give it to you as a gift, Maha? Would you accept it?"

While cheerfully checking the necklace, he discovered that Old Man had made a pocket in the middle square, "good for a love letter"—that trickster Old Man!

Imad stuck the report in the small pocket and placed the necklace back on the nail next to the lamp, and went back to his notebook and his pen. He cheerfully wrote:

I ran after her bright butterflies,
I forget what I said.
A talk between a prisoner and a visitor, fragile
like fluffy scattered wool.
We each said random words,
agreed, commented, but didn't say much.
My ears heard your unspoken words,
They made the mighty birds sing!

They said all that wasn't told!
I said nothing!
I didn't put my colored feathers on display,
like male birds do,
still I looked for a glance from you.
You had a glory-laced presence,
I looked at you and gazed.
Your voice ran through me,
rivers of milk and honey!
The agate in your chain glittered,
when you bent over the window's wire,
a feminine sweet letter.
Your innocent glance made me shiver.
How sweet was thinking of you here!
No prior date between us made,
no secret glances behind parents' backs,
no silly, dull smiles,
just a "hello" that put you high,
in my eye your shadow sat,
light as a butterfly.
No makeup, nor colors, nothing false.
Your presence took me by surprise!
With no permission, every step you took,
guided the pulses of my heart!
You left, but with you, I stayed!
Your fiery hair,
Your bright, rosy cheeks!
The tiny freckles on your face,
your pointed little nose,
and your ever present smile.
The twinkle in your hazel eyes,
the beauty of your figure,
your image all together,
music calls tenderly!
I followed your scent, walked aimlessly,
away from the clutter of the days,
from the whistles of the guards,

and the clamor of the place!
Between two forces you appeared,
a small Chrysanthemum flower,
the size of the agates in your ears.
The flowers swept away
the darkness of my day.
I peeked calm, marginal, but poised.
A flower, smaller than the button
holding tight your clinging shirt,
over a firm flowering chest
canceling places, times, and dates.
The inmates, rushed, stopped, then walked,
nothing but your shadow remained,
with strong feelings of loss and gain.
Generous, you walk with me, in the prison's yard,
your shadow stretches inside my veins.
I saw nothing but your steps leaving,
far beyond the prison's walls!
My life changed from that moment on.
Countless times, I thought of you!
How sweet it was to think of you!
Glorious the beautiful sunset came,
bringing with it a promising dawn.
How tender was the Eid's crescent,
painted, an eyebrow on the sky!
As if I discovered beauty this evening!
As if I saw the world for the first time!
As if I swam into the clouds!
As if . . .
As if I loved her again, and again!

The sky over the prison seemed wide open, filled with jasmines, floating in the air like happy butterflies. (*The Little Prince* said, "The fundamental and important is not seen by the eyes of old people.")

He slept a little, dreamed that he was a bird in a jasmine bush, and then saw himself standing at the prison's wall, with his arms wide open. He stretched his neck and felt it covered with feathers, flapped his arms, and heard The Cat calling, "Fly, soar . . ."

"My feet are heavy."

"Extend your legs and fling your body."

"I can't."

"Imagine yourself swimming, Comrade. Swim, Comrade."

"I will fall and break into pieces."

He saw the guard at the high tower pointing his gun at him. He lost his balance, fell, and flapped his arms.

The Cat called again, "Fly, soar high, Comrade!"

He soared and heard the bullets coming at him. He woke up frightened, and saw the guards blocking the entrance of the White House.

It was a search!

The white room was not usually subjected to random searches like the other wards. This time, the white room was the target—in particular, the Comrade! They checked the mattress, ripped open the pillow, examined his papers, drawings, and books, page by page, looked through his clothes, one piece at a time, and checked all pockets and creases. They took the books, drawings, and papers; during all of that, his mind was racing. He knew what they were looking for; he knew that Judas was one of Christ's closest disciples.

"Thanks to the Old Man for the beautiful necklace, and damn The Cat . . ."

While they were leaving, the officer pulled the wire off the lamp, yelling, "This is also not allowed."

The electricity stunned him!

"Ha, ha, ha," laughed Tuj.

Sergeant Younis slapped him on his face and continued his search. They went through the room quickly and confiscated Hassan's radio, Abu Nazmi's knife, and condoms that no one admitted owning. The officer asked, surprised, "What is this for?!"

Sergeant Younis looked at the Minister and told the officer while stretching out his lower lip, "What about trying on each of them to see!"

His Excellency's cheeks swelled; his face became red; his breathing turned to snoring.

Suddenly, the Engineer screamed, terrified, "Hey, Your Excellency! Mr. Minister! You!" They carried him to the prison clinic, but he did not make it to the hospital alive!

Irbid

The rhythm of time became regular again. The students went back to their classes at the school over the hill, and the nightmares of the dungeon and walking on the edge of the prison's wall returned. He missed the simple nightmares he used to have when he was in school. Then, he would dream that he went late to his exams, or that time passed before he finished them. He missed being at the university; he missed Irbid's mornings, the aroma of the freshly roasted coffee, the smell of fried falafel, and the fragrances of the mixes of perfume at the attar shop.

Since Maha came into his life, his sense of time changed. Nights suddenly became long, and he paid no more attention to the sound of cars behind the prison. He had time to daydream.

The street was the same, but not like it was in Ramadan. It was not crowded anymore, and had no more lanterns and decorations. Children stopped playing with their marbles in the neighborhood alleys.

Walking in the moonlight in September was refreshing. He had the urge to continue wandering in the streets until the sun rose.

The Souk was the same, but after midnight, it looked like a stage for creatures that were invisible in the busy day. The hallmarks of the city changed. A small, obscure grocery store was lit and frequented by sleepless taxi drivers, on-duty police officers, and desperate smokers in wrinkled pajamas, looking for cigarettes to buy.

On the side street, the city sanitation truck was collecting the garbage from the bakery while the workers were preparing the dough for the next day's bake. Meanwhile, Umm Kulthum's voice sounded. "He kept saying things to me and I kept saying things to him, until there was no more talk."

At night, more cats appeared. Around the corner, a man with tattered clothes searched in a dumpster and placed his finds in a makeshift cart that he had constructed out of wires, scraps, and wheels. In the alley, a young boy on an old bicycle collected empty cans. The sounds of people at night differ from the sounds of those buying and selling in the daytime.

After midnight, the upbeat popular songs disappeared and were replaced by melancholy old songs of Umm Kulthum, Abdul Wahab, or Abu Baker Salem.

When dawn approached, the big trucks sped through the main streets they were not allowed to travel on during the day, hauling their goods on their way to faraway places, followed by heavy machines deployed to different construction sites, and then buses on long-distance trips.

When the parties ended at University and Thirtieth Street, the customers left the restaurant. Café owners hurried to clean their shops and wash the entrances in anticipation of new customers. Meanwhile, downtown Irbid woke up to the smell of falafel fried at the small shop at the corner of Prince Talal Street. At the crossroads, the drunken, the dwellers of the night, the workers, the farmers, the soldiers going early to their posts, and the teachers on their way to faraway schools, crossed paths.

Abu Salem's cart appeared ready to provide coffee and tea with its lit Primus that filled the air with the smell of gasoline. The Farouq, the peddler of sesame bread, boiled eggs, and other condiments, was ready to sell his load. The fragrance of fresh pita and tannour bread on its way to supply Yasin and Qasimiah restaurants filled the place.

The city went into a frenzy in the morning. The sidewalks were crowded with plastic tables and chairs full of customers waiting for their breakfast, hummus, falafel, ful, onion, olive, and a lot of freshly baked bread. Those who found no chairs took their plates and sat anywhere, on large water bottles or on sacks full of beans in front of the shops, and ate their breakfast. At the western corner of the street, sandwiches were rolled out in a hurry to feed the hungry masses gathering in front of the window of the Ahmad Falafel shop. Meanwhile, Teyrawi's juice stand quenched the thirst of those crowded at the eastern corner of the street.

At dawn prayer, he saw the believers coming out with their white thobes and wet flip-flops on their way to the mosques, followed by the daily workers with their baskets and axes scurrying to their jobs, chatting along the way.

The city calmed down after dawn prayer, allowing time to see the moon depart and watch the soft clouds of September pass through the horizon changing formations, followed by a crisp, clean wind. With the first sunrays, the birds started their busy day singing, and then left looking for their daily sustenance. Their songs were quickly replaced by the loud noise of people, public transportation, private cars, and school buses. A new day started with new possibilities.

How beautiful is the morning!

He missed the school's bells and the national anthem, "Lives the King, glorified be his station . . ." He missed the newspaper peddler selling his papers, reading the headlines, "Beirut is ablaze, the King goes on a quick visit to Oman, the tomato crisis in the Jordan Valley farms."

He missed the fresh produce market that stretched from Mameluke Mosque to the west of the Big Mosque to the east side of the city, with its vegetable vendors competing in rhymes:

"The figs are coming, they are coming; from Rahoub come the figs."

"Light and sweet the cantaloupes."

"From Hawara the pineapples."

"Red and pretty the tomatoes, from Rehab come the tomatoes."

He missed the calls of the peddlers in the second-hand clothes souk, yelling:

"This skirt for the pretty lady."

"Make your son happy for ten gersh."

"This slip for the hip."

He missed people walking through the crossroads.

He missed the university bus and the hearts pierced by arrows drawn on the back of the seats.

He missed the Writers Society in its humble headquarters behind the post office building. He missed the poets and their arguments, the writers and their gossip, and the artists with their disheveled beards and hair. He missed al-Qayrawan, the post office, and the university circles. He missed the street corners where they sold lottery tickets, and the narrow alleys where they mended shoes. He missed the scribes, sitting under their large umbrellas filling out forms, drafting letters and requests. He missed the peddlers spreading their merchandise on the sidewalks of crowded streets, tripping passersby.

He missed Irbid's evenings with their light clouds, their bite of cold, and the dust from the midday sandstorms rising with the clamor of the city all the way to the top of the hill.

He missed al-Camal's coffee, Afouri's sweets, Durzi's hummus, Yasin's ful, and flipping through the books and magazines at Zarein's bookstand.

He missed Sheikh Khalil's bus station, and the loud call, "Last customer to Amman, last soldier to al-Zarqa be ready. Let's go."

He missed Irbid in the evenings, when the workers from the villages returned to their homes, the loud bustle of the city vanished, and men gathered in front of their shops and their houses to smoke and drink tea with mint.

He missed the black and white stone houses with bougainvillea bushes by the walls. He missed the basil, the mint, and the coleus with its velvet leaves at the windowsills. He missed the passion- and honeysuckle-flower vines covering its fences, jasmine and grape trellises in their entrances, and the chrysanthemums growing between the joints of their rocks.

He missed the vendors walking in the streets and narrow alleys selling sesame bread, cotton candy, and other cakes and sweets.

Like the peddlers, his mind roamed the city's streets, looking for her home, using what the Engineer had described to him one day when he was in a good mood.

He found himself with her, filling his lungs with the fragrance of the evening jasmine, when Irbid gives up its noise and lounges by the hill, content to be a quiet and serene city!

He missed Maha . . .

Did he love her?

(When my head glows with joyful thoughts, I wish I had a golden pen, and silk papers to write my words. They did not write the Mu'allaqat with gold water to gloat. They did that to crown the joy the writers felt when creating them. Hanging these poems at the Ka'ba's wall, the point of adoration of all Muslims, it was for nothing but to bestow happiness and be generous to man!

(Unfortunately, the glow of happiness is short-lived. When life giveth happiness in one hand, it giveth in equal sadness and misery in the other. This happens even in prison.)

The Nude's Island

For all things there are starting points, and for desires, there are doors, keys, and guards. For the prison bath, there was a door, a key, and a guard. The key of the bath was in the hands of "Abu Zaki Canary"; he supervised the schedule, the cleaning, and the maintenance of the Primus.

The bath was rectangular with a domed roof; it had one window beside the door and a skylight in one corner of the west wall. Below the skylight in the corner was a fireplace, and on top of it a barrel of water. A Primus replaced the wood that used to feed the fireplace in the past. The southern wall was split into five sections separated by barriers, each only one meter high. The barriers were low so they could watch inmates and deter any temptation. However, sin is elusive, insidious, chooses its victims and picks its time. Here, the inmates discover each other's nakedness. It does not only expose hidden imperfections, covered scars, and embarrassing tattoos, but also reveals strengths and beauties.

It is a place where people bare their souls, where hearts are wide open, and nudity matters not. Here masturbation is not a secret habit. Young inmates compete in who can spew his sperm farther. Here the gays choose their partners, even if only imagined. The first time he entered the nude bath was on the day of his arrival at prison, with Asaf, who bragged that his was bigger.

After moving to the White House, he had the privileges the "elite" had and was able to bathe alone, enjoying the benefits of being with his body without a watchful eye. Abu Zaki Canary reserved Wednesday for the elite.

Today, due to the large demand on using the bath caused by a number of unexpected additions to the White House who wanted to bathe, Imad went in with Hassan. He chose a corner far away from Hassan, got some hot water and poured it over his body, scrubbed his head with the soap, rinsed it, and scrubbed his neck and back. When he reached his midriff, he lathered it well and it became spontaneously erect. He closed his eyes recalling her image, Maha's image, but he could not. Hassan called to him, interrupting his thoughts. Hassan could not see well without his glasses. He asked Imad to hand him the soap that had slipped out of his hand while bathing. Imad picked the soap off the floor and noticed Hassan's uncircumcised organ. He touched it with the edge of the soap and laughed, "You have an extra handle!"

Hassan took the soap from Imad and said, "You laugh at it!" He then reached out and held Imad's and said, "Wow, stiff!"

Their bodies touched, tempted by the warmth and the smoothness the soap lather left behind. They were enthralled by pleasure for a few seconds, enough for Abu Zaki Canary to catch them in the act! They were both in one stall, naked, laughing!

How embarrassing, what a shame!

They did not realize that they could have bribed him with what would have guaranteed his silence—until it was too late. Atalla Baik was informed and found it a chance to humiliate the Comrade!

He ordered them to strip, painted their midsections with molasses, and hung them on the window of the White House for all prisoners to see. How harsh was the sun! How slow was the dirt worm caressing his skin and going through his pores one at a time! Oh, how heavy was the fly; and even the butterflies rushed to partake of the displayed feast!

Damned are the *Zogrut*!

How far did that bee travel to get its share of the taunted nerves!

Wasps, ants like smooth sesame seeds, fireflies, dragonflies, and miserable butterflies with straw-colored wings, all came. What did they eat before this public feast!

How heavy were the beads of sweat, forming, dripping, and burning the nerve endings!

The worst was not over. The insects fiercely feasted on his exposed skin, making his body cringe; his soul trembled from the chilling shame, and the pain caused by his stripped ankles and wrists was suffocating. He had difficulty swallowing his defeat. Even when they tied his big toe to his penis, and he thought about giving up, he had not felt defeated!

Hassan screamed, cried, and asked for mercy. Meanwhile, Imad clenched his teeth, stared at the sky, and felt broken. There was no one there to defy and win against, no idea to defend or a Party whose secrets needed protection; just a prisoner being punished for a foolish act. He felt defeat and betrayal, and in his soul, a desire for revenge escalated; perchance it would make him feel vindicated.

All around him, inmate faces were staring, terrified. Behind him stood the guards, smoking and chattering to hide their feelings. Such a penalty was sufficient to feed the prisoners' nightmares for months to come and intimidated both inmates and guards. It enhanced the status of Atalla Baik in the eyes of his superiors, and tightened his grip on his subordinates.

They untied them after an hour. It was longer than Mischa's day!

Was the worst behind?

No. It had just started.

(Only if the young man is a stone, the troubles would pass him by, and he would stay still unaffected.) [38]

The prisoners did not stop gossiping about him; each made up his own story! Guess who is the "honey" and who is the "butter?"

"He is a Communist with no morals and would sleep even with his mother!"

"A gentleman, what gentleman!"

The prison turned into a beehive.

Damn the *Zogrut*!

He felt a volcano of tears rage inside him, and he lost the fragrance of jasmine from his memory. The howling of the wolf in him turned to agony, and the white house became dark and gloomy.

He went on torturing his soul and stopped thinking of Maha. He was too embarrassed to see visitors, let his beard grow, and grew a light mustache that made him look like a student in high school. He stopped going to the bath, stopped having wet dreams, and no longer masturbated.

The body that used to heal with a sprinkle of salt became sensitive to everything, and the superficial wounds on his wrists and ankles took a long time to heal. He hated Canary, managed to avoid him, and spent his night crying silently.

The isolation was painful, a constant agony that started at dawn.

What was the point of confrontation if man breaks and engages in trivial and insignificant fights?

Did the sheep eat the Little Prince's flower?

Man can handle being destroyed, but not defeated! What if the Old Man in *The Old Man and the Sea* were falsely accused and became the laughingstock of the fisherman, he who conquered the arrogance of the sea?!

.　.　.

The Cat and the Old Man succeeded in pulling Imad from his isolation. The Old Man remained faithful in silencing the rumors, shutting the gossipers up and exposing their own faults. The Cat continued to nurse the Comrade until his wounds healed. The Old Man took him to drink tea at Tamouni's Café. "Your friend, The Cat, is brave. He attacks anyone who speaks ill about you."

The Cat stopped by and said, laughing, "We will cut the tongue that speaks ill about you, Comrade; your reputation is more honorable than he will ever be."

The Old Man pushed him jokily. "Go shower and stop blubbering."

The Cat turned his head toward the White House and threatened, "You will see, Canary will kneel at your feet; just wait."

The Old Man scolded him. "May God the Great forgive you! Go away, Cat."

Just mentioning Canary's name stirred the desire for revenge in Imad's heart.

The Old Man sensed that and tried to keep him away from trouble. "I am here, Comrade, because I was possessed by the demons of revenge!"

.　.　.

The solidarity that his friends demonstrated helped Imad come to terms with his problem and reconcile with Hassan. In solidarity, they faced the vicious rumors and became friends, but his reconciliation with his own body took much longer!

His view about the people around him changed: Some rose in his esteem, like Asaf, who considered it a tribal matter and defended his cousin; Mr. Marlboro, who ignored the whole incident; and Tuj, who did not change his behavior toward the Comrade, even though he was not able to hold his tongue in a few incidents. Others fell, like Abu Haddid, who found in the incident a confirmation that all humans were immoral by nature. Meanwhile, the trustee of the ward, Nazmi Abu Hashish, with the loud noise he produced when smoking his water pipe and the rude comments he made, combined with Abu Zaki Canary avoiding them and showing indifference, made their life miserable.

The Engineer was busy following up on the development of his case, but he listened to Imad with attention. "I am human, just like Hassan. Hassan's problem ended when the physical pain subsided. Why do I suffer so much, as if I am the keeper of man's morality?"

The Engineer smoked his pipe silently, and his eyes filled with tears. "What is the path to happiness?"

■   ■   ■

His experiences taught him to be steadfast, to compete and confront. This helped him emerge victorious in the end. He defeated Nazmi Hashish by ignoring him, and made his animosity toward Canary explicit by putting him down.

The bees stopped buzzing, his wounds were healed, but his agony did not stop!

He got up, took out his notebook, and drew an elephant inside the belly of a snake and a sheep grazing on baobab trees.

He glanced at the faces of the inmates of the White House! What a misery! They had no depth; he saw them as mere shapes and sizes! He drew the White House and discovered that it inspired nothing but darkness. He threw the pen away, rested his elbow on his notebook, and went on watching the prison courtyard under the moonlight. At night, the prison looked spacious!

■   ■   ■

In the morning, a thick bundle of sunrays streamed through the window. Hashish reluctantly handed him part of the newspaper, and Tuj brought him his cup of coffee from Tamouni's Café.

He turned the pages of the morning paper without concentration.

He paid attention and heard the sound of a fight coming from the prison courtyard.

In a few minutes, blood spilled and bones smashed. Canary was standing in front of the bath watching the fight, enjoying the scene, his belly shaking while he laughed! The vein under Imad's collarbone shook, waking the wolf inside him. He jumped, light as a lynx, across the battlefield. He tripped on Asaf, who was lying on the ground, fell on top of him, and kneeled to get up, to find his face looking at Canary's belly. A razorblade that someone placed in his hand glittered, and he attacked like a wolf, stabbing the blade into Canary's neck with quick, angry, precise strikes. Canary fell, wheezing like a slaughtered sheep. The inmates backed off, spewing vulgar curse words, words that we all know but have the decency not to include when we write.

One of the mobs won, and the other lost. Faces and necks were slashed and clothes were torn. Asaf was on the floor, his face covered with blood, and Abu Haddid holding his hand, spitting out his own broken teeth in his other hand. Imad's hands were dripping blood, his shirt ripped, exposing his left shoulder, and Canary was lying on the ground, wheezing, slaughtered. The prison's alarm sounded! In a few minutes, the prison was on lockdown, the wounded prisoners transferred to the prison's clinic, and many sent to the dungeon. The juvenile delinquents appeared with their plastic buckets and tall brooms and washed the floor.

·   ·   ·

Typically, bloody disputes were expressed by using razorblades. It was the most common method among the *Zogrut*. The blades were small, sharp, gave quick results, and were easy to handle. The experts hid them stuck to the roof of their mouths. Razorblade wars were common in prison, like tattoos that have their expert artists, who mix ashes with glue and hammer using bundles of needles until it settles under the skin in a complicated ritual that is both painful and comforting. All that was needed when it was all done was a blessed handful of salt sprinkled on the surface wounds to dry them. The professional prisoner bragged about these cuts and slashes, just as he bragged about his tattoos! In their view, it symbolized self-control and saved the soul from feeling defeated! Perhaps it was a symbol of having a certain freedom, a symbol of power! The sacrifices of generations of prisoners succeeded in gaining this minor privilege and acknowledging its rituals without a written contract.

The Engineer sat next to Imad at the entrance of the White House.

Imad looked down. "This is the first time I used a blade. A strange feeling took over me while I was stabbing Canary's neck, the blood gushing out and splashing me. Will I turn to an expert in this and tattoo my arm with a head of a wolf or a jasmine flower, for example?!

"Abu Zahra, who handed me the blade, praised the skill with which I used it. I would like to say to him, 'Abu Zahra, it was probably the power of revenge and not the skill of a professional.'"

The Engineer explained, "There are knives for fighting locally made from a cover of a sardine can or the handle of a spoon that is folded and sharpened by a rock for many days until it becomes a tool capable of stabbing. If someone had handed you a knife, you would have killed the man. Do you hate Canary that much?"

"Now, I pity him, a broken man."

"Here he is sitting in his corner, hiding his wound with a large red keffiyeh."

Fighting is like a game, a human need that is not only for a certain age group, or people from a certain social class. On the other hand, blood is dangerous, addictive, like cigarettes, drinks, and hashish.

Many here smoked cardamom, ate ants, and sniffed glue. Some even inhaled the fumes from the sewage until they got dizzy. The alcoholics drank cough medicine or medical alcohol that they stole from the prison's clinic. They sometimes smuggled in a tray of sweets drenched in wine instead of syrup, which smelled with time, like the stench of old used socks. The secret was addiction, and most prisoners were addicts! Addicts who continued to commit the same stupid mistakes any way possible. The petty thief was used to picking pockets. The robber was used to stealing, the rapist used to rape, and the homosexuals preferred men. Even the ways these habits were practiced were perpetual addiction; each person had his or her special way of doing things, like a fingerprint!

"Is addiction pleasurable?"

Neither the Engineer nor Imad had an answer. They remained silent.

"Revenge is pleasurable," said Imad.

■   ■   ■

The tribes of Imad and Canary outside prison raised hell because of the incident. They sent *Jaha*, a group of distinguished and influential men, to each tribe to intervene, and dispensed *Atawat*,[39] and at the end, they drew a tribal reconciliation deal between the two parties.

Imad did not get as much support from the members of his own tribe when he was arrested. But because of this incident, the tribe's wise leaders were proud of him, and warned him of the revenge the victim might plot against him. Young men visited him in prison and enthusiastically and openly boasted about their solidarity with him.

"Why?" Imad asked.

"Because you are brave, you fought and won, and made us proud—not like Asaf, who lost with his head down with shame, inside and outside prison."

Then in his tribal people's eyes, he and Asaf were the same. The difference was that he was the brave "aggressor" and Asaf was the weak and "deceived." Ha, ha, ha. They did not like to say "loser" or even "victim." The son of the tribe is always a hero and loses only by being deceived! They deceived us in the 1948 War; we did not lose, but they even deceived us in 1967.

For a whole week, tribe members of Imad and Canary did not stop visiting!

Imad delegated the Old Man to represent Imad to the victim's family, and Canary delegated Abu Ganani to speak to Imad's family. For tactical reasons, Asaf was considered Canary's victim, which led to making the peace accord easier, and the case was closed.

. . .

In the tense atmosphere that followed the battle, the only pleasure he had was reading. He went back to reading what the prison authorities allowed—sorry, the Authority of the Reform Center, as it was now called. He read books as if they were tasks that had to be accomplished or a destiny that had to be fulfilled. He read quickly because the prison authorities frequently pulled back books in order to make the point that everything was under their control. For that, he read *Sahih Al-Bukhari*, *The History of Jobarti*, the letters of Ibn Taymia, and *Al-Umm* by Al-Shafie. They did not allow him to have *That Scent* by Sunallah Ibrahim. Their objection was that "Sunallah" literally means "made by God," and since God "creates" and does not "manufacture," the book was censored! They would have prohibited the novel *The Gambler* if it were not for the new head of Interrogation, who gratefully wanted to show how cultured he was, and wrote, "Just a novel, does not harm or help. Written by a non-Communist Russian author."

How do things go? "I am with Asaf, and Asaf with Abu Haddid, who is against Abu Ganani. My friend The Cat with Abu Ganani and Abu Zahra handed me the blade. Canary was the victim. Help me understand, Old Man! From where did Kurzum bring the metal bar that he used in the fight?"

The Old Man laughed. "Abu Ganani hid the bar before he left the prison two years ago. When he needed it, he knew who to get it from."

"Why was The Cat beaten by the prison authorities?"

The Old Man answered, "He was the one who kept the iron bar."

"In the sewage?"

"Yes, you are good."

The Old Man laughed and said, "Your feathers have not grown yet. You have much to learn, son."

"I don't understand!"

"The Warden called him and said, "You have to give our man his pride back, otherwise . . ."

"And he gave up? Damn him."

The Old Man laughed, "He was a donkey, like you."

Imad was surprised. "You, Old Man, call me a donkey?!" He was angry.

The Old Man realized that what he said angered Imad and said, "I meant a wolf, by God a wolf, a daring wolf."

Imad was not ready to hear more. He left the Old Man and went for a walk, aimlessly.

He was not able to sleep that night. He stayed up, asking himself, "Am I a donkey?"

It was not what the Old Man said, but that prison does that: it always tests us; it exposes us.

By dawn, the fragrance of jasmine spread into his heart. He tried to recall Maha, but failed. He only remembered the freckles on her nose. He yearned to go to her, to the university, to his house, to his mother and father. He thought about "recanting" again. He thought about the paper that he had written a while ago and forgotten. It seemed from a very distant time. He saw it as a wall of silence that blocked the prison gate. He turned his face away from the wall, picked up a pen, and tried to write something. His brain was flooded by images, the "cage of the circus": a tiger, cat, wolf, snake, camel, lizard, The Cat, and himself, all crammed in a square; no escape for the wolf, no den for the snake to hide in, and no place for the lizard to lurk at and wait for its prey.

He asked himself, "Who am I in this cage?"

So many imagined that they understood him and knew his secrets, the secrets that he himself did not understand. Often they reduced him to one word, "Communist," then placed him on a shelf in their mind, just as the pharmacist does with the bottles of medicines.

"Who is capable of turning the mist into statues and monuments? The Old Man said it, 'A donkey!' I am a donkey, and if I accept the compliment, I am a wolf!"

He drew himself a wolf with a donkey's head, with two long, wide ears. He laughed. "The heart of a daring wolf and the stubbornness of a donkey."

The Reconciliation

Asaf saw Imad, stopped by, and said, "What a brave man, my dear cousin; when we leave here, you have my dove."

"Your dove!"

"The white one, my car, the Volkswagen."

Imad laughed, imitating Asaf's lisp. "Your car? Go away!"

Asaf left and Imad turned to Abu Haddid, consoling him: "The fight is over and no one died, Abu Haddid."

Abu Haddid collapsed, crying, "I have been unlucky from the day I was born, Comrade. I wish I had died when my mother was burned."

He told Imad, sobbing, "I was told that I was born on a hot, dry day, and on that day, my father died. When the midwife gave him the good news about my birth, he was overjoyed. He ran to the closet and took out a gun that he inherited from my grandfather, which he had never used before. When he tried to shoot it in celebration, it blew up and killed him. After a year and a half, the Primus blew up when my mother was warming water to bathe me. She was burned and the neighbors saved me. I lived with my maternal grandmother, and when she died, I went to live with my paternal uncle. I was in the fourth grade, and I never went to school after that, not because I am lazy, but because I am an orphan. My uncle took me to Ajloun to tend his herd of goats. When I got older, I asked him to give me his daughter's hand in marriage; he was furious and kicked me out. I moved to Irbid and worked as a porter in the market until that gloomy day. I never delivered to people's homes. I used to load and unload full truckloads by myself, but fate led me on that miserable day to load furniture. They asked me to load it on the truck, and then asked that I go with them to unload it at the house. There was a woman there, by herself. She annoyed me with her endless requests: not here, there, move it to the right, put it there, in the corner. She slipped while she was wiping the new end tables. I jumped on her; she scratched my face, but I raped her. They sentenced me to fifteen years. It was the first and last time."

His tears poured down his face.

"The prisoners dream of all sorts of women, in all types of positions. The deviants dream of young boys, and I, Comrade, since I entered the prison, I only dream that I beat a woman and rape her. I have never seen a naked woman, and I never dream about women except in torn clothes. Even when the story of Karma and The Cat circulated, I could not imagine the matter but as a rape. I dreamed that she was hung by her hair from the ceiling with a rope that I controlled, reeling her up and down. Even in my dreams, I rape women!" He wept bitterly.

Next day, Abu Haddid was transferred to Ajloun prison, as he requested.

Abu Ganani took the place of Abu Haddid, and Kurzum returned as the trustee of the North Ward.

After the reconciliation and admissions, Abu Ganani came with The Cat to visit the brave man Imad in the White House.

Abu Ganani was a perpetual liar. His choice of the hoopoe to tattoo on his shoulder befitted him. He did not make up realistic lies, but big lies. He humored the Comrade by telling him that he loved artists and writers. Imad showed him one of his paintings. He looked at it, shook his head, uninterested, and said, "Read us some of your stories."

Imad pulled a paper out of his bag and with the enthusiasm of an amateur writer he enthusiastically read, "The straw: With it the bird builds his nest, and it can spoil a drink. The wind tosses it around, and it could start a fire in a large forest. The straw can break the camel's back.

"A snake attacked a bird; it held a long straw with its beak; the snake had a hard time swallowing the bird; the fight between the straw and fang lasted for some time. The bird had a chance to win!"

Abu Ganani said, laughing, "I liked your paintings and did not like your story. The story that does not have a lie that shakes the listener is not a story."

Imad said, "But that is a symbolic story, and not a tale; imagine a straw in a person's mouth."

"Ha, ha, ha, you brag about lying? Nice!"

"This is a story, not a lie; there is a difference."

"The story is a lie, but people believe it. When I tell the truth about myself, it is perceived as a lie. That is why I keep the truth to myself and give people damaged goods. I lie. Ha, ha, I am the winner."

The Comrade turned his attention to The Cat and teased him: "You came out of the feast with nothing; instead you got a beating and spent three days in the dungeon. Nothing changed. Here we are, still the same."

"Ha, ha." The Cat laughed from the bottom of his heart and continued, "How could I have flown if I had all that heavy weight?"

The fragrance of jasmine spread into Imad's soul, and he felt two soft wings flutter inside him.

Maha

He knew that she was coming. He hesitated, but then he decided to go.

He saw her by the visiting screen, carrying a jasmine between her forefinger and her thumb.

She greeted him first.

He answered warmly.

She said enthusiastically, "I participated in a sit-in at the university."

Her father was busy talking to her mother about contacting the authorities regarding his release. He was not listening to her conversation with Imad.

They were comfortable talking. As the conversation went on, they became intimate. He was fully aware of everything she said, every gesture she made. They talked about so many things. Did the people around them stop talking? Their talk was becoming increasingly intense and intimate. It separated them from the world around them. The room felt like a "merry-go-round"; new channels of joy opened, breaking any residues of reservation between them. Her mother did not seem to object; she looked at them with approval. They did not stop talking, despite the whistle of Sergeant Younis announcing the end of the visit.

She said, "It's as if we've known each other for a thousand years."

". . ."

"We are dressed up the same, jeans and a white shirt and tennis shoes!"

". . ."

"By accident, or it's meant to be?"

". . ."

"I want to drink Rahoub water"

". . ."

"I knew you before you knew me."

". . ."

"I saw your picture in brochures flying around the university asking for your release."

". . ."

"They would quickly disappear."

". . ."

"If one of the flyers about you escaped the censorship of the university guards, the students were afraid to pick it up, and whispered to each other, warning, 'prohibited flyers.'"

". . ."

"I gathered my courage and picked up one. Placed it among my private things."

". . ."

"It is still there."

". . ."

She laughed, changing the subject. "If my father goes to court, many of the people at the top will go down with him."

". . ."

"My father will be let go soon."

". . ."

Then she went back to talking about him. "I bragged to my friends that I knew you personally."

". . ."

"I would love to see your paintings."

". . ."

"I would love for you to write to me."

". . ."

"A jasmine flower."

". . ."

"For you. Didn't you say that you liked jasmine?"

The flowers of the jasmine bush inside him flourished, and he felt its fragrance stretch through his veins.

Imad recalled every word she said and sailed deep into her hazel eyes, wavy red hair, the opening of her white shirt over her firm breasts, the color of her shining black belt tight around her skinny waist, and the degree of blueness in her tight jeans. He recalled the shadow of each smile, the movement of her bangs, every freckle around her nose; but he could not remember what he said or did.

He walked around the prison courtyard with the other inmates that were walking around, with one thought on his mind: "Will she visit me next time?"

"Why should she visit me? Because I was wearing a white shirt, and blue jeans, and light shoes? Ha, ha, ha.

"She will not visit. Why would she subject herself to security threats?

"But she gave me a jasmine.

"I will give her the poem I wrote to her after I met her for the first time, 'As If I Love Her.'"

He did not feel The Cat walk next to him until the whistle blew, announcing the return to the wards.

The Cat put his hand on Imad's shoulder, who bent a little to come down to his level, and said, "Be assured, she also loves you."

They both laughed.

■   ■   ■

At the White House, the Engineer seemed happy, and two days later, he was released.

Imad and Hassan walked him to the interior gate of the prison. The Engineer seemed hesitant while shaking Imad's hand, then turned to his bag, opened it, took out a white envelope, and handed it to Imad.

"To whom?" Imad asked, confused.

"Take your time reading it," said the Engineer.

Imad opened the letter and read:

I do not know if I love this boy or hate him.
    I do not know if he is my rival or my image.
    His presence confuses me.

Perhaps he does not know what changes he brought to the White House and its seven residents. With him there, we compared him to ourselves and ourselves to each other. Our conversation became elevated, and our behaviors refined. Prison had meaning, time grew important, and morality gained strength.

I do not know what he thinks about us, but we in the White House were much lowlier before he joined.

If I let my imagination soar, I might say that His Excellency the Minister died from indignation. This indignation would not have been possible if it were not for his agitating presence. Just comparing his "crime" with our sins was an instigation.

Oh, Imad, if you only knew!

Perhaps we went against you because you exposed us to ourselves.

Perhaps we hated your presence, but we loved you despite ourselves.

Perhaps getting used to something is the source of human idiocy. With time conscience sleeps; why did you wake it up, my son?

Should I apologize to you on their behalf? Were we too cowardly to side with you?

This is not enough, it is not an apology or regret; we faced you in a way that helped us assert ourselves, by insisting on our stupid actions.

The defeated man is afraid to bring up his true convictions; he hides behind fake masks an emptiness that makes him unstable. With time, he gets used to disappointments and covers it by justifying what he is now.

When I was your age, Imad, I was a zealous Communist. In Moscow, where I studied engineering, I was a strong supporter of the Party, and the Soviet Union, and the ideas of peace and socialism. When I returned to Jordan, I denounced the Party and went with the current. I would not let an opportunity pass without making fun of the Party. I did that not because I was a bitter critic, but because my past was haunting me. The apostates are the fiercest in attacking their former beliefs!

Slow down; do not think that my confession is a sign that you led me back to the right path, and that I will get back to the ideas that I abandoned a long time ago, and beliefs that I left behind . . .

What I want to say to you is this: Who betrays his soul once cannot trust himself with anything.

Do not betray your soul, my son.

■   ■   ■

With the death of His Excellency the Minister, and the release of the Engineer, the prestige of the White House decreased, and the influence of its residents on the administration diminished. It became a transit station for the relatives of local officials who were put in prison for a few days for random crimes such as traffic accidents, shooting in celebration during weddings, or tribal disputes. On some nights, they would even make a path in the middle of the room and have transit detainees sleep there.

All of this passed while Imad thoughts were floating in a different realm.

After her father's message, he felt she was closer to him. He drew her with a cobia pen, running at Rahoub's vineyards. He smiled when he saw her image that he had drawn, took out the dried jasmine, and talked to her.

"She loves me, doesn't love me.

"Why should she love me?

"She loves me.

"She loves me not.

"The jasmine was playing tricks on me."

Mad

The Cat came to Tamouni's Café not feeling well, sat with Imad, who ordered for him a cup of tea and a Kamal cigarette. The Cat did not want the cigarette, so Imad smoked it and asked The Cat, "Don't you have work today?"

The Cat asked for a little more sugar, dissolved it in his cup, took a big sip, and said, "Your friend is tired, Comrade."

"Sorry to hear that."

"I couldn't fly last night; all my dreams turned to nightmares."

The Comrade laughed. "What a shame! Who will fly over Irbid and tell us how it's doing?"

"My back, my back is killing me, Comrade."

"Karma broke your back, ha, ha."

"Oh my back!"

"..."

Imad took his friend to the health clinic.

"My back, doctor."

"Do you have any other complaints?"

"Everything hurts."

The Comrade pleaded, "Please take care of him, Doctor."

"Why? Is he special, or have you recruited him to join your Party?"

"Please; if something happens to him, who will dream for us?"

The doctor laughed. "You don't need a doctor; you need a psychiatrist to understand you."

The Cat groaned. "Please doctor, I can't fix faucets."

The doctor looked at the guard and said, "It might be a disk; we need to get an X-ray."

The man opened The Cat's file and said, "The Cat does not leave except with a pardon or dead." He then looked at him and continued, "Here is your file; we did not forget the kidney stone, Cat."

The Cat said, pleading, "Please, I have only a few months left; I am not going to try to escape."

The guard said, "Go away!"

The Comrade said, "You will be responsible if something happens to him!"

"Heck, a minister died here and nothing happened."

The doctor looked at the Comrade and said sympathetically, "I wrote him a transfer to the hospital, and the rest is the hands of the Warden."

The Cat put his hand on his ear and started singing a popular song, "The iron softened, but you didn't / if you knew his condition, you would have softened for sure."

The doctor was pleased with his sweet voice!

The guard said, "Your voice is sweet, but your silence is sweeter. Go away, Cat, we need to handle others."

The Cat left with the Comrade, and Hassan went in.

■   ■   ■

Imad walked around the prison courtyard more than ten times, and suddenly The Cat took a step back, stretched his arms, stood on his tiptoes, opened his nostrils wide; his smile widened, and he danced.

"You tricked me; you are not sick!"

"The trick didn't work. I miss the streets of Irbid."

They laughed hysterically.

Imad imitated him. They stretched their arms, opened their nostrils wide, smiled, tapped the ground with their toes, balanced, waved their arms, and joyfully danced, indifferent to the inmates who gathered around them, making sarcastic comments.

"They've gone mad!"

"What did they drink?"

"What did they sniff?"

"Ha, ha, ha, ha!"

"Crazy!"

The Cat clapped his hands with a beautiful rhythm. The audience clapped, then the voices calmed down, and the rhythm became more regular, "tra, ta, ta, trat, trat, tro."

Soft mist poured down, fueling the enthusiasm of the audience, and The Cat sang, "I am afraid I loved you and adored you / and love threw me right into your house / We flew each night, and still miss each other each night / tell our story, O evening bird."

Joy was infectious and filled all corners of the prison. The courtyard was flooded with inmates. The whole prison was affected by the contagious madness. Even the five ward trustees and the guards in the towers danced; yodeling was heard from the women's prison.

Rain poured down, but no one cared.

The celebration continued until the whistle of the guards sounded, calling on the inmates to go back to their wards.

Imad walked out of the dance circle into his own happiness.

He wrote to Maha:

Your visit untied the knots in my soul. Turned waiting that blazed inside me into a raging forest fire and gardens of flowers.

You are my heaven that I carry inside me, wherever I go.

I started walking in this bewitched place, in my eyes light, and in my feet determination.

Morning is near and you are far away.

You are near and the morning is far.

You are far and the morning is far.

Winter Returns

Winter returned, and the cold wind carried Fairuz's warm voice, singing, *"Winter returned, keep thinking of me."*

Winter returned, and Mr. Marlboro was released and went back to work for another ministry. Al-Sadat visited the Knesset in occupied Jerusalem. Abu Canary made other unsuccessful real estate deals and defaulted in one of them, so his opponent took him to court, and his release was delayed until a decision was made in the new case. This greatly affected him, especially with the endless comments and sarcasm he received from the inmates.

Asaf was moved to al-Zarqa prison, even though he had only one month in his sentence, because he conned the prison warden himself. He had submitted exaggerated reports about the amount of gold the prisoners had in their possession when all they had was a small amount: a ring, a chain, a coin. Then he convinced the Warden that he could gather the gold for him from the other prisoners for very little.

"I hope it is not stolen, Asaf," warned the tempted Warden.

Asaf told the Warden, revealing his plan, "Stolen, borrowed, robbed, all that you should care about is making a profit. The penny will make two pennies in a couple of weeks!" Asaf sold the Warden a kilo of fake gold.

The Warden did not dare to open a case against Asaf, and instead he transferred him to another prison. Everyone in prison knew what had happened. There were no secrets in prison; even Imad's story with the Engineer's daughter, who continued to visit him after her father's release, was known to all.

Imad was busy with her and did not pay them any attention.

The Little Prince told him, "If you love a flower in a star, it is wonderful to watch the sky at night. All the stars will be flowering. Important things can't be seen; they can be felt."

■   ■   ■

Winter returned, and Eid Aladha was back. It had been a year since Imad was sent to prison. Today, it seemed so long ago. In that time, the streets, the schools, the university, and the villages around the city seemed remote. His village, Hawara, was an hour's walk from the prison and five minutes by car, but it was far away now. All the places that were familiar and intimate seemed distant today. He wondered, "Was I really there?"

Winter returned; the days became shorter and the nights longer. Djibouti joined the Arab League; the Comrade was happy that Amnesty International won the Nobel Prize for Peace, because they used to send him greeting cards that ended with the phrase "Keep your thumb high." Abu Canary's television broadcast a program about the death of the "King of Rock, Elvis Presley" by a drug overdose, which scared the drug addicts in prison.

Winter returned, and a rumor spread among the prisoners again: "A royal pardon is near." Prisons are often emptied each new year.

He became aware that the rumors of pardon were nothing but the foam of buried aspirations, but he used this cruel "illusion" to relieve the bitterness of his days.

Winter returned, and December arrived with its harsh cold and drenching rain that changed the pattern of the noise coming from the cars going up and down the hill.

Winter returned, and the rainy days increased; the sunlight became scarce. Maha continued to visit him every Tuesday, and his mother visited him every Friday.

■   ■   ■

Imad recalled . . .

My mother's visits were great. She talked to us about the house, and the jasmine bush, the harvest this season. I asked her about my father's patio, and she scolded me. I talked to her about details; we talked about the uncles and the aunts, and the grandsons and granddaughters. "Your sister had a child, and she named him after you." Her eyes glittered with a childish joy when she added, "There are now seven boys in Hawara that are named after you."

She did not say much, but supported me in her kind, motherly way. She frequently would say, assuring me, "No one can take off your head, except the one who placed it there."

I touched the beaded necklace in my pocket. I almost told her about Maha, but I did not find the right words.

The visitors' line for men was much longer than that for women at the door of the prison. My father arrived late and wet. I greatly respect my father. He greeted me warmly, and we talked about world events before moving on to Arab affairs and ending with talk about our village politics.

Hassan, the Old Man, and The Cat came to greet my family. My father talked to them kindly. He asked Hassan how much longer he had to serve.

Hassan said, "I was sentenced to twenty-seven months, I finished twenty and have seven left."

My father said, "Time passes. It will end before you know it." Then he turned to The Cat and said, "What about you, Saeed?"

The Cat laughed. "Three months, by God, I will enjoy these months." He put his arm on my shoulders and continued, "I won't leave without this cub; he's coming with me."

My father laughed and turned to the Old Man and asked a different question, avoiding the length of the sentence, knowing that he was in for life. "How are you doing, Abu Muhammad?"

"Thank God, well." The Old Man gave a signal, and they all took off so that I could spend time alone with my father.

My father moved back a couple of steps and slowly drank his tea, allowing my mother to get closer to the screen. She reached out through the window and touched my face, shoulders, and checked my clothes. She always said that I was skinny and that I did not dress enough to fight the cold. It was her way of telling me she cared.

■　　■　　■

Tel Irbid was built by man over five thousand years ago. Traces from the Bronze Age, the Hellenistic civilization, and then Greek, Roman, and Islamic were found in its hill. The Saraya building, where the prison is now, dates back to the reign of the Mameluke. Within its walls, they sorted the ice blocks brought down from Mount Hermon, packed and shipped them to Egypt. When the Ottomans came to the region, they rebuilt the Saraya—the platoon residence, during the reign of Suleiman the Magnificent—according to plans made by Sinan Pasha (died 1580), and it became the symbol of their authority in the area. This was confirmed by the Swiss traveler Burckhardt, who passed by Irbid in 1812. After Ibrahim Pasha left the Levant in 1841, the building was neglected again. Later, the German traveler Schumacher in 1884 described it: "An arch towers over the front entrance, which leads to a square courtyard surrounded by lines of stone rooms built with limestone and basalt. By the entrance, a number of steps lead to the second floor. The building, overseeing the surrounding plains, shelters shepherds, bandits, and farmers during the winter."

When the Ottomans spread their control over Irbid and the surrounding areas again, they repaired the building and made it in 1866 as inscribed on the stone they mounted by the exterior gate today, a prison and center for the gendarmerie.

Thinking of history took him back to the cellar.

He wondered if walking in the tunnel, as The Cat described, would lead to discovering the layers of history in its depth or would just get him out.

He started imagining himself crawling in the cellar and seeing light at the end of the tunnel. A light that would lead him to endless cellars. The journey consumed him; it became the subject of his nightmares and daydreams.

He decided to enter the cellar and sneak through the tunnel, where he would either find a treasure or a way out, or perhaps he would disappear like the young Imam and return when it is time to fill the land with justice and equity after the wave of injustice and wrongdoing that consumed it.

This time, he voluntarily sneaked with The Cat to the prohibited area by the exterior gate of the prison. They stood there watching Irbid at sunset, sending its people back to their neighborhoods and villages. If they saw them there enough times, their presence would become more acceptable. Officer Younis asked them gently to get back in.

The Cat whispered, smiling, "I told you; they are getting used to it."

Imad said, "I wish I could sleep in the cellar."

"Why?'

"To see the tunnel, enter it."

"You want to escape?"

Maha's image flashed in his mind, a bright butterfly.

The Cat looked into Imad's eyes and said, "Do you love her?"

He replied joyfully, "Yes, I love her, I love her!"

He returned to his bed at the White House, elated with the words he had said, feeling that he had passed a barrier that he feared. To think about her, to count the freckles on her face by rote, to recall her soft neck, and the golden chain hanging over the bright opening in her white shirt, put him in a mixed state of apprehension and desire.

He said, "I love her," and heard the echoes of his words reverberate inside him. He turned the light on, took a piece of paper, and wrote with large letters and pretty script, "I love you," and placed it in the pocket of the beaded necklace.

■   ■   ■

She sat silently, recalling his image of running around joyfully, giving water to the people by the visitors' screen. The dignity and honor that she detected from his spontaneous act, and the humbleness he displayed in picking up the empty paper cups, made her respect him. His tender smile when she gave him one of the cups and what that smile did to him are hard to describe. It was as if the water of Rahoub in these paper cups was pure love poured into her heart.

She held his fingers in her soft hand and looked with her hazel eyes into his soul, and told him, "I love you, and I proudly say it again, I love you."

They said nothing and let their imaginations soar high to Rahoub Spring, the plains of Huran, the mountains of Ajloun, and the rest of their homeland that welcomed them with an open heart. They ran with the wind, soared in the sky, sang with the birds, and rested under the shade of the flowers. Joy filled the place; the prison screen turned into meadows, and the prayer beads with their bright colors transformed into beautiful flowers.

The bell rang, announcing the end of the visits. She gave him a bunch of jasmine flowers and a small book that she pulled out of her notebooks, careful not to let the guard see it, and gave him back the beaded necklace!

■   ■   ■

He took out her letter from the necklace's pocket, looked for her scent in it, and read it time after time with a hazel joy. She wrote:

After my first visit to you, a fine stream of Rahoub's water poured into my memory. You walked with me in Irbid streets and went with me to the greens at Yarmouk University. I bought a sandwich and a cup of tea and asked the boy at the counter to pour it for me in one of the paper cups that you gave me at prison. I sat under the fig tree, across from the manmade waterfall where you told me you used to sit. I was not able to recall your features, except the way you bent to talk to me at the visitors' screen and the blemishes in your face. I know that I want to see you again, and I thought to bring you the flower you like. I talked to you in my mind, and I imagined how you would tell me about your love for me. I prepared my response down to the smallest detail, including the way I would move my bangs. Your presence poured into my soul like the water of Rahoub that quenches the thirst, like the shade of the fig tree loaded with desire, and a waterfall that resembled yearning.

Why was he reading it time after time; had he missed something in the previous readings?

After two or three nights, he was not sure. When they turned the television down, he pulled out the book and read. The fragrance of jasmine filled the place.

"Oh, how beautiful is the Seagull![40] If he were not in love with Maha, he would have fallen in love with her just for introducing him to this Seagull.

The hardest, the most important, and the most enjoyable flight is flying to the worlds of love and discovering the meaning of tenderness.

"Oh, how much I love you, Maha!"

"How wonderful you are, Richard Bach!"

It is enough for man to think about what he wants and want to be there bad enough, intensely and honestly, for it to be a true reality.

He slept with the book in his hand and saw his lover between the layers of two clouds basking in the milky mist. They danced with the white clouds, soared with Jonathan the Seagull, and ascended with the dew deer. They slept over the jasmine leaves and placed their heads on its soft white petals.

He woke up feeling her, and the scent of jasmine spread in his soul like a miracle.

It seemed that he had found the antidote for his soul sickness. The book did to his skin what the ointments and pills failed to do. His allergy went away, and he was able to use soap again. The book became his companion and occupied a significant part of his conversation with her when she came to visit.

She said lovingly, "I dream about translating this book one day!"

He held her hand through the bars and said, "My love."

He could not wait to get back to his corner to get the paper out of the necklace. He took it out as soon as she handed it to him, spread the pink paper decorated with flowers, and read, with no concern for the curiosity of the crowd next to him at the visitors' screen, what she had written:

> How beautiful is the writing! How tender are the words! His eyes flood with love and kindness. When he bends at the visitors' screen with a yearning to talk to me, I get a strong urge to embrace him, and kiss his handsome, blemished face. Sometimes, I wish I could hold him by his thick curly hair and say to him, I love you Imad. I shouldn't tell him that I love him; he should say it to me first . . .

He laughed, "What is this, Maha? I must have been an idiot not to see!"

She held his hand and said, laughing, "I wrote it during a boring lecture."

The beaded necklace continued to travel back and forth between them each visit, and Jonathan the Seagull flapped his wings and continued to be present, perfuming the flood of their emotions with the scent of jasmine and fueling their longing with the promise of freedom. Through all of this, the necklace was the witness that carried their longing for each other and their burning desires without attracting attention to them. Beaded necklaces and similar items were commonly exchanged at the visitors' screen.

■   ■   ■

Imad woke up early and wrote:

> Tuesday, the beginning of December 1977
>
>   I woke up at 5:30 to write to you.
>
>   Light drapes the universe, and gives the prison some of its splendor.
>
>   A bird picking at something behind the window. Prison birds are all the same.
>
>   I did not know if he was the same bird or if it was another. Only one bird comes to my window at a time. It chirped and flew away. I sent you a "hello" and a smile with him. I was going to tell him about you, but the noise from a passing car made him fly away. I did not see the car. The window was much higher than the street. If you passed by Hassan Kamel School, you might have seen the bird hopping around on a roll of barbed wire, waiting for you.

At 6:00 a.m., the doors of the wards opened, and the inmates poured into the courtyard. In six hours, I will see you. How slow will the next 360 minutes pass?

I drank coffee, read the newspapers, and read the horoscopes before I read Bader Abdul Haq's column. I did not care about what the horoscopes said; I saw when I worked at the newspaper how they randomly copied it from other papers. However, when I read your horoscope, I feel an intimate connection to you. I also looked at the prices of vegetables.

Now, I have to take a bath, shave, and get ready, cherishing the minutes I wait for your arrival.

I love you.

He took the "recanting" statement out of his notebook, read it quietly as if it belonged to someone else, crumpled it, and threw it in the garbage can by the door. A joyful light spread through his chest, and he wrote cheerfully,

I love the jasmine, I love the poppy flowers, and I love Rahoub Spring. I love blue, the color of the sky. I love the Little Prince, and Jonathan the Seagull. I love The Cat and Old Man. I like football, Pablo Neruda, Aziz Neysin, Emil Habibie, Salvador Dali, Goya, Jawad Salim, Sadi Yousef, and Kazantzakis. I love Fairouz and my mother, and Abu Moussa and my father. I love Marcel Khalife, the Path Band, Abdul Halim Hafez, Rumi, and Khayyam. I love the clouds and the moon. I love 'Arrar and Wasfi al-Tal and my grandfather. I love Ho Chi Minh, Castro, Abdul Nasir, Hawari Bu Median, and my brother. I love sparrows, doves, and flocks of Abu Saad birds. I love Budapest, Aqaba, Hawara, Alexandria, and Tunisia. I love my aunt Amina, my uncle Salim, my first teacher Nadia Abu Rahmoun, and my sister Naifa. I love Ghawar, Anthony Quinn, Muna Wasif, and Abba. I love Dostoyevsky, Walt Whitman, Hemingway, and Ursula Andress. I love Surat al-Rahman, the Song of Solomon, and the Psalms. I love walking. I love the rain. I love the night. I love the morning. I love olive oil, bread, milk, and mallow. I love savoring the taste of things. As much as all of that, I love you.

From one Tuesday to another, the letters became longer: one, two, three pages. The pocket in the necklace was not big enough anymore.

She greeted him with her soft hand. He noticed that the knuckle of her middle finger was inked and a little swollen. He commented, "Studying hard?" She replied, "Writing to you," and they both laughed.

"We went out in a protest against Sadat's visit to Jerusalem." She looked taller and older than her age.

" . . . "

"We closed Theater Street downtown." He wished that he was there to protect her.

" . . . "

"You are going to get new Comrades; take care of them." She sounded like his sister.

" . . . "

"The Comrades recruited me." He felt that she was far away.

She said with a childish joy, "I asked them to do so." Her eyes were laughing, and lost their glow.

She expected that would make him happy, but he felt that something heavy had landed on his chest.

At the end of the visit, he said goodbye to her with sweating palms and teary eyes.

This time, the necklace carried a different kind of paper:

Private: A Special Report to the Advanced Cadres of the Party

On 9 November 1977, Sadat made a bold statement before the Egyptian Parliament when he announced, "I'm ready to go to the end of the world for peace, even to the Knesset itself." Ten days after that, Sadat visited Jerusalem. He abandoned the Geneva Convention and the approach to achieving a comprehensive peace. Sadat's visit to Jerusalem caused chaos and split the Arab world. Some Arab leaders endorsed the initiative, and others opposed it, while many chose to wait to better assess the situation.

The Arabs will not be able to restore their rights if the effort to liberate Arab occupied land and reach a just peace is unilateral, partial, or committed to a unified Arab position.

Sadat speaks about breaking the psychological barrier, which was, according to him, 90% of the Arab-Israeli conflict. With this, he sees that peace is possible without Israel's withdrawal from the occupied territories! Sadat did not succeed in conquering the political barrier to peace, specifically Likud's refusal to withdraw from the West Bank. In this regard, Sadat's visit failed.

He burned the report and thought about Maha. What if she was placed under surveillance or expelled from the university? Would he consider himself responsible for what happened to her? He started thinking of her as a sister, a Comrade, and remembered a story the Comrades circulated about a Bedouin Comrade who wanted to marry, so they suggested that he marry a particular girl from the Party. He answered them indignantly, "Be ashamed, you are terrible, she is a Comrade, and that is incest!" He laughed, and then quickly became sad thinking about the Comrades recently arrested, which she mentioned during her visit. He imagined them tortured, beaten, and placed in solitary confinement. He wondered who would resist and who would give up. The taste of injustice was stiff, bitter, and hard to swallow. He thought, "For how long will this go on?"

∎   ∎   ∎

On Friday, his brother came to visit.

". . ."

"When the police attacked, I ran away."

"I am glad; what would happen to my mother if they caught you?"

His brother laughed and commented, "She says that it must be an evil eye. That we seem to be among those who deserve 'his anger.' I told her, 'Mother, isn't that better than being among those who 'went astray'?"

They laughed.

"I saw Maha in the demonstration; she is a brave girl."

The Comrade put his head down and did not answer.

"What? I thought that you would be elated?"

"She is too young for demonstrations."

"Why? The first time we went out, we were younger than her."

"Honestly, I don't want her to get involved in politics."

His brother said, "This is selfish." Then he laughed and added, "This is backward."

Imad argued, "When you knew that my sister had joined the Party, you were upset."

"I was upset because I didn't want her to become Communist like you."

"You mean a Party member."

His brother laughed and said, "You're right; it is the retardation genes that we inherited. We need time to get rid of them."

He returned from the visit full of questions.

The idiom *Getting beaten by sticks is not like counting them* is not true. His body shivered and ached when he thought about his recently arrested Comrades, who were probably going through the interrogation and torture that he went through when he was arrested.

The pain oozed out of memory and burned his soul more intensely than when he actually experienced it. Now, his mind was saturated with details that he had not fully comprehended when the experience actually took place. Now, he realized that true pain comes from recalling the scenes, with all the details, cursing, slapping, spanking, flogging, roasting, suspension, the nylon thread, isolation, and the bitterness of prison and its surprises.

"Oh. My tooth!"

He tried to sleep, but he was constantly interrupted by the toothache, or the recurring nightmares that haunted him. He saw his friends subjected to flogging, roasting, and suspension, and ran away panicking. Then he found himself in the tunnel, touching the wall, a stone at a time, in search for a loose stone, his skin shriveling with desperation. He saw his friends smiling, happy with their handcuffs. He rose to meet them, raising his thumb, but ran into the prison gate, trembled when facing the silencing wall. He woke from his sleep, panicking, and felt a rash spread throughout his skin.

The pores of his skin became needles that poked him day and night. The bird Jonathan was unable to lull him to sleep anymore.

The prison doctor examined him and mumbled something to the nurse: "Scabies."

He tried to convince the doctor that he was not suffering from scabies, but allergies. The doctor dismissed him and said mockingly, "Are you a doctor? Why don't you come and sit in my place!"

They rubbed his skin with sulfur, with its nauseating odor that added to his anguish, and placed him under quarantine in one of the isolated administration rooms at the second floor.

He felt more isolated than he had ever felt before, not even in solitary confinement. The itching bothered him more than the bees had when he was suspended with molasses on his body. Suddenly, his toothache overwhelmed all his other pains.

Next day, he could not distinguish which tooth hurt him the most. All his teeth hurt as if they were connected to an electrical wire.

The Pasha intervened and got him permission to see a dentist.

He passed the gate for the first time since his trial, checking the gates, the locks, and the spaces between the two gates with interest, as if he were looking for a missing rock in the wall.

The doctor took the needed safety precautions and opened the patient's mouth wide, placed the saliva extraction tool under his tongue, and started criticizing the Soviet Union for not supporting the Arabs against Israel, as it should, and cursed Communism, as he understood it. Meanwhile, Imad was thinking about Jonathan the Seagull.

Jonathan was not a Communist, but he lost his right to speak and was expelled from the herd because he discovered that flying is freedom. He had to pay a price for that sin!

The doctor finished his work and sermon and prescribed two aspirins as needed, and he recommended that a dermatologist examine him.

The nurse from the dermatologist's office came, took a sample of his inflamed skin, and sent it to the lab.

That night, in his quarantine room above the wards, the effect of the anesthesia went away, "Oh, my tooth!"

Isolation and toothache made him think of the purpose of his life. He felt that he had lived for a long time, as if he had grown ten years in one year!

He thought of the riots taking place at the university and worried about Maha and his detained friends. When the superiority of the opponent is overwhelming and decisive, the victim has nothing but the straw to protect him from being swallowed.

When he was debating with his friends at the university, he would extoll the steadfast, brave ones with a romantic enthusiasm, and relentlessly described the ones that gave up and recanted as falling and disgraced. Today, he understood the plight of each. He did not see them as equal, but understood human frailty.

We resist together unified, but face abuse and torture alone, each according to his spiritual capacity.

He took a deep breath and said to himself, "Each is responsible for his own actions. Take two aspirins and go to sleep . . ."

He saw Maha fly with him between the clouds, bathe in their soft, transparent moisture, ascend with the dewdrops, and lie on the flower, with her red, fiery hair flowing on her face. Suddenly, he collided with the prison door and found himself in front of a solid wall.

The lab report saved him from his isolation. The prison doctor admitted that Imad's skin inflammation was an allergic reaction, but he did not prescribe steroids because "it was not allowed" in prison.

He went back to his bed and pillow in the White House, picked up *Jonathan Livingston Seagull* from under his pillow, and opened it. The scent of jasmine spread. He randomly flipped the pages; he had already memorized the book.

> Once there was a seagull named Jonathan, who was growing up without growing old. His capacity to fly tremendously increased, and he became spectacular. He flew and flew farther and faster. One evening, Jonathan was surprised by the arrival of two transparent and radiant seagulls with wings made of light. They took him to the land of seagulls that really knew how to fly. He discovered that behind his skies there were other skies, and that there was endless knowledge of aviation that was much more than what he knew.

His veins pulsed with the yearning to discover a sky farther than the space above the prison, with a desire to soar, to fly to the land of seagulls that really knew how to fly. His toothache became unbearable, and he screamed, "Oh, my tooth!"

He took two aspirins and went to sleep.

∎ ∎ ∎

When the pasture became green, the herds fell ill and could not enjoy it!

The year 1977 was almost over; it was Tuesday, but she did not come. Had something happened?

He shaved twice, played with his pimples until they bled, burned his face with cologne, changed his shirt twice, and spent a long time getting ready. The visitation time was almost over. He sat disappointed at Tamouni's Café, thinking of her, imagining her breath touching his soul with a moist tenderness. Thinking of her by his side sent a sweet chill through his body.

Hassan's voice interrupted his sweet daydreams. He was startled, as if someone was spying on his thoughts.

"Where are you, man? You have visitors. They have been calling you."

He quickly gathered his scattered thoughts and ran, almost tripping from joy.

It was not her, but the Comrade that brought the reports from the Party. He said, "A new wave of arrests!"

"Because of the riots?"

"Because of Sadat."

". . ."

"Is there anything you need? We will not be contacting you for some time—you know, emergency."

"And Maha?"

"They forbid her to visit you."

"Who? Her parents?"

The Comrade's silence had the taste of sand.

"Who? The authorities?"

The Comrade said nothing, then took a deep breath and said, "The Party."

His visiting Comrade pulled the jasmine bush out of his veins. He mumbled what his father had said about the government a year ago. "Screw this Party." The Comrade pretended not to hear that.

Oh Cat, I wish I could borrow your voice and scream, "Oh, Oh, Oh!" until the sky opens and swallows me.

The Cat

Had a day passed?

Getting used to things kills time! When he asked Old Man what he meant by saying, "Don't get used to prison," Old Man laughed, and then sighed with regret. "We learn only from our mistakes." He repeated the Sura: "By eve time, Man is at a loss."

He walked alone in the courtyard, aimlessly, under the rain. The Cat sneaked and walked next to him in circles around the fountain. He did not object. He actually hoped that he would say something that would take him out of the depression that the Party's decision had caused, but The Cat remained silent. When the sun peeked from behind the cloud, shielded by clouds, The Cat picked up two chairs from Tamouni's Café, closed because of the rain, pulled Imad by his sleeves to a sheltered corner, and sat across from him.

Imad smiled. "Good news?"

"Comrade, do you want to know who The Cat is?"

Imad raised his eyebrows, inquiring. Honestly, he was thinking of Maha and had no desire to hear anything about anyone else, but could not say that to The Cat. The Cat rested his elbows on his knees, supported his jaw with his fist, and went on speaking with eloquent and refined speech, as if he was a student reciting a memorized poem; meanwhile, his colored hair was dripping water, a drop at a time, like orphans' olives, scarce and slow to be offered to others.

He said:

> When I was young and innocent, I had a kind mother who cared for me and saw the light of the world through my eyes. I used to love words and songs. My mornings were at school, my middays at public libraries, and my evenings with books spread out at the street corner. I used to return to my mother with bright words like shiny, finished clay figures . . .
>
> I was born like thousands who are born every day to this world, because a poor man walked up to a poor woman one day and poured in her the bitterness of his harsh life.
>
> I grew up like thousands who grow up feeding on sunlight and drinking the rain. You find young, sad men hanging at the corners of sad streets, and you wonder, how did they grow up and become tall and strong, with the meager life they had!

Then he continued answering the questions revealed by the Comrade's look. "You know, Comrade, some time ago, I used to love words."

His wet locks fell on his face, and he continued, "When I was young and innocent, I had a kind mother who cared for me, and the light of the world shone through my eyes. She saw me as the most handsome and the smartest among my peers. I used to love words and singing them. I spent my mornings at school, my afternoons at public libraries, and my evenings at bookstands on the streets, and came back to my mother in the evenings with shining words like shining treated clay."

He took a deep breath and added, "My mother used to enjoy my orations and see them as sweet as honey. Her eyes, her cheeks, her dimples would all smile, and her voice would sing, as if I were hearing it today, 'May God protect you, and make you live long so that I can see you as a teacher, a judge, a governor, or a rich man . . .'"

He moved his hair off his face and said with a sad voice, "But I became a thief!"

Imad's eyebrows arched in sympathy, and he said nothing . . .

The Cat wiped his tears with his thumb and continued avoiding the surprised eyes of his Comrade. "My mother was a maid who collected leftover bread and scraps of clothes from the homes of wealthy people she worked for, and I did nothing but occupy myself with useless words."

He continued. "When I was busy with nothing but that hopeless nonsense, my mother fell ill, became an invalid, and died."

He was silent for a second, then said, "Did she die of hunger? No!" He took a deep breath and added, "My mother did not die of hunger! She lived hungry. As a result, she got sick in the morning, her health failed her by noon, and she died before nightfall."

He then sighed, with tearful eyes, "She left me with nothing but a shack and a mulberry tree."

They were interrupted by the guard's whistle announcing the time for The Cat to get his tools and go to work. With teary eyes, Imad stroked The Cat's hair and said kindly, "This is from Salah Abdul Sabour!"[41]

The Cat said, choking on his tears, "You are right, Comrade, but Abdul Sabour was wrong; this is my story, not the story of Halaj. Hunger can turn one into a beggar or a thief, but hunger does not make a rebel."

Then he laughed between his tears and said, moving the locks of his gray hair off his face, "I chose to be the latter. Stealing is more honorable than begging. Ha! My interpretation!"

Imad held The Cat's hand with sincere affection. "I learned a lot from you, my friend. You taught me happiness, and today, you taught me—"

The Cat raised his finger, interrupting. "All the prison learned from you, Imad. You changed us, brought out the nobility in us. You reminded me that I have wings!"

Imad's eyes filled with tears, and The Cat laughed and said, "It will all end soon, Comrade."

But trouble in prison never ends.

The Secret of the Dungeon

" I was at the Souk, and I stopped to see you."

His father used to visit him sometimes on days other than the visitors' days. He had a natural reverence that opened doors for him wherever he went. This made him a natural leader. The committees formed to advocate for the rights of prisoners selected him to speak on behalf of the families of political prisoners, which infuriated the authorities.

Atalla Baik decided to assert his authority that day and prevented the Haj from entering the prison. He pretended that he was expressing the authorities' dismay with the Haj for crashing the opening session of the National Advisory Council and presenting the issue of political prisoners in Jordan, then distributing to the media a list with the prisoners' names, sentences, and how long they had been detained. His father asked one of the guards—he knew him and respected him—to take a bag of oranges to his son. Atalla Baik came to the door and said arrogantly, "We said, 'not allowed, Haj; go away from here.'"

The father felt humiliated, threw the bag of oranges at the Warden, and said, "To hell with you!"

The news quickly reached Imad with added incitement, "He threw the Haj out."

"He threw the gift down the stairs."

"The Haj promised not to visit the prison as long as Atalla is in it."

"Don't let Atalla, the lowlife, get away with this."

What will the Comrade do?

He went out to the inside gate and saw Atalla standing between the two doors, yelling and screaming . . .

"This is chaos; everyone drags behind him his 'abaya and walks in here . . ."

The Comrade interrupted him, yelling back from behind the gate, "Atalla, do you think you are as honorable as the Haj? If you are a man, come in here . . ."

Atalla was taken by surprise, and the prisoners intervened, pulling the Comrade away from the gate.

The prisoners spread the story, exaggerating Imad's reaction and diminishing the Warden's. The guards talked about the oranges that rolled down the stairs, and to make the story more exciting, the prisoners embellished it by adding that one of the oranges continued to tumble down the hill, crossing the main street and stopping at the vegetable market by the farmer that sold it.

The day passed without Atalla entering the prison.

The Warden did not enter the prison every day; sometimes weeks would go by without any of the prisoners seeing him; but as soon as the prisoners entered their wards, the whispering started. "The Warden is afraid of the Comrade; that is why he is not coming inside the prison." The next day passed, and the gossip increased. "Atalla is a coward."

The gossip reached the Warden and the Comrade, and they both felt cornered.

If the Warden entered the prison, it would be perceived as a late and meaningless response to a challenge made by a helpless prisoner. The prisoner was in a tough spot too, because there was not much he could do if the Warden came into the prison.

On the fifth day, Atalla came to the prison, accompanying a health committee that periodically visited prisons for a routine check.

The Comrade was walking back and forth in the prison courtyard with fast steps, as all prisoners around the world do, when the inmates gathered around him, agitating him. "Here he comes . . ."

"Go to the son of . . ."

"Kick him out like he kicked out the Haj."

The Comrade sat by Tamouni's Café and asked for a cup of coffee in an attempt to avoid an embarrassing situation. The Warden came in with the committee to check out the kitchen. Imad breathed a sigh of relief, and then he saw the committee head at Tamouni's Café with the Warden behind him. His veins pulsed and the wolf inside him woke up. He stood and raised his voice. "You dare to come here? You are an asshole, Atalla!"

The commission retreated, and the Warden was stunned; his face turned yellow. Some of the prisoners gathered around the Comrade, and one of them handed him a short stick. He felt the jar of fear shatter inside him and pour boldness into his veins. The Warden ran away towards the gate. The Comrade could not remember how all of this happened, but he saw the stick fling from his hand and hit the Warden's lower back. Atalla wobbled and almost fell; two guards held him and they went out of the gate followed by the commission.

The emergency bell sounded, and the prison was placed on lockdown.

Kurzum carried the Comrade on his shoulders, celebrating, surrounded by the prisoners singing in celebration, "Our hero, our groom, the pride and sheikh of all men."

The guards on the wall left their machine guns and lined up, waving at him, smiling . . .

At that moment, he saw the prison as a forest of jasmine, and he felt more than any other time that he could fly.

The guards led him to the dungeon as if they were leading a groom in his wedding procession. It became clear to all that Atalla was hated by the guards more than he was hated by the prisoners.

That was his chance to examine the tunnel in the dungeon. He bent and crawled as The Cat described, and suddenly the tunnel became dark and narrow; he could fit only his arm through it. He stretched it all the way and decided to widen the opening. He started moving the soil enthusiastically. His lungs filled with dust, and his breathing became heavy. He lay down quietly and enjoyed the darkness and silence of the tunnel away from the main prison and its clamor, the city and its noise, and the government and its ways. He was in a good spot in his life—everyone loved him; nobody that mattered to him hated him . . .

He fell asleep and saw Maha in his dream holding a jasmine, and his mother yodeling, releasing the jasmine flowers, filling the sky.

He heard a distant wolf howl.

He woke up . . .

He felt the dirt that he had dug leak out, and smelled rotten air coming from the depth of the hill. When he traced the movement of the dirt, he saw that it was leaking through a hole at the bottom. The leaking hole exposed an opening as wide as a small plate. He gathered the dirt around his hand and poured it into the hole. He wished he had a lantern to see where this hole at the end of the tunnel led to.

"Did it lead to freedom, or to the dark secrets of this ancient hill?"

If Jonathan discovered the sky beneath the sky, maybe he would discover the ground beneath the ground. He would win one of two victories: reveal a secret, or find a way out.

He questioned the possibilities: "Do you plan to get out of this hole, walking in the city like this? You would run away; who do you think you are? Do you think you are capable of escaping and running away forever? You fool; they will come after you from café to café, from street to street, until they find you."

The soil stopped pouring into the opening. There was nothing left but darkness; and in this darkness, he thought of the promised one who would fill the world with justice and amity, instead of the injustice and contention that covered it today.

In the midst of my pride, I did not care if the tunnel sent me to oblivion forever.

He woke up to find himself in the hospital, surrounded by police, doctors, and his family, even his uncle the Pasha.

His eyes looked around, searching for Maha to no avail.

■ ■ ■

Atalla Baik was transferred to border patrol, and his father started visiting him again as often as he could. The dungeon was sealed with cement, and the hill kept its secrets. The tunnel became a tale that prisoners told the fresh newcomers.

Things changed; the new warden humored him, the residents of the White House went out of their way to appease him, the inmates rushed to serve him—but Maha did not come.

Unexpectedly, his bad luck struck again. The residents of the White House were talking about the Engineer and how lucky he was to move with his family to America!

His brother confirmed that during his visit the following day. "After the embezzlement case, migrating was a good option for him and his superiors."

"And Maha?"

His brother shrugged his shoulders, confirming what he thought was a given. "Of course he will take his family with him."

Suddenly, Maha appeared, at the visitors' fence . . .

She came with all her glory and impulsive braveness . . .

She came like the water of Rahoub that quenches the thirst . . .

Like the shade of a fig tree full of desire . . .

Like a waterfall that resembles longing . . .

She stuck her arm through the bars, held his neck, stood on her toes, and passionately kissed him. She was full of pride and indifferent to the staring eyes of the inmates, the guards, and the visitors.

"I will be back, my love. I will plant for you a jasmine bush wherever I go. I will translate *Jonathan the Seagull*. I will finish my studies and return. I will write to you from there, I will always write . . ."

His heart broke! She acted as if she belonged to her new world before she even got there. Would she remain faithful? Would he stay faithful?

"I don't say goodbye; we shall meet again!"

He returned from the visit, "crying and laughing, neither happy nor sad; like a lover who drew a line in the sand."[42]

He asked to be transferred to the main prison . . .

The Cat laughed. "Prisons are the same, even if they are at the shores of the Riviera . . ."

No Way Out

A year and a half had passed since Imad's arrest.

Winter came, carrying its heavy load; cold scorched the walls and stung the bones. The Commission for the Centers for Rehabilitation and Reform agreed to transfer Imad to the Central Prison in Amman as a hopeless case. The clouds dropped their heavy load, and the rain fell in sheets. It kept the inmates in the wards. They did not come out for the midday count; instead, counting took place inside. Meanwhile, Imad packed his bags, ready to leave for Amman in the morning.

Despite the storm, Imad's friends gathered to throw him a goodbye party at Tamouni's Café.

Rain in prison has a mellow rhythm that evokes memories. No sound is more beautiful than the sound of rain, whether falling over a Bedouin tent, or pouring from the gutter of a mud house, or tapping on the glass of a classroom window, or dripping over jasmine flowers by the entrance of the house, or pouring through the drains of the prison.

The opening at the end of the gutter stirred a flood of feelings and memories . . .

(Are there high gutters on the roof of Amman Prison?)

The Cat filled a teapot with water coming down the gutter, and Old Man started a fire at a dry spot in the corner of Tamouni's Café, which was closed because of the rain. A few of the friends gathered, taking shelter and warming up next to the fire. Abu Zahra brought a ball with tea and sugar and dumped it in the teapot. The Cat leaned on the wall and sang an old song: "The iron softened, but you've never showed love; if you knew how much he suffers, you would have definitely shown love."

He sang rich, melancholic melodies to the rhythm of the cracking cold drops of rain . . .

They drank their tea with the raindrops bouncing and splashing their faces . . .

Everyone was silent in reverence when the call of Assar prayer was heard . . .

The Old Man wrapped his keffiyeh around his head and tied it over his iqal, and performed his Assar prayer while splashed by the raindrops running off the prison wall.

Abu Zahra fed the fire with the scraps of wood and flammable items he could find around.

Kurzum asked The Cat nervously, "Are you sure Asaf is out of Zarqa Prison?"

The Cat nodded his head, confirming . . .

Old Man turned his head right and left in supplication and said firmly, "Is everything ready?"

Imad said, "What is ready? What are you whispering about?"

The Cat drank the last drop of tea in his cup and moved on to sing another song:

Oh, Oh, Oh, Oh father.
The Judge tricked us and made us sign a pile of papers,
Oh, Oh, Oh.
We managed prison, and patience stayed,
Oh, Oh, Oh
Who could help us deal with fate!
Oh, Oh.

Old Man's tears fell and mixed with the raindrops, forming small rivers running down his wrinkled face. Kurzum picked up the empty teapot and filled it with rainwater, while swaying with the melody of the song.

The Cat leaned toward Imad and said, "Forgive me, Comrade!"

Imad laughed. "For what?"

"The paper."

"Which paper?"

"I didn't understand the gravity . . ."

"What are you talking about, man?"

"When I told the guards about it."

Imad looked into the teary eyes of The Cat and placed his hand over his shoulder kindly. He was surprised about how serious The Cat's expression was, so he said nothing.

Kurzum came back, carrying the teapot full of rainwater.

For no reason, Old Man scolded him, "This is mud, not water, you dummy!"

Kurzum slammed the teapot into the wall, screaming, "I'm not dumb, you jerk!"

The Old Man kicked the bucket in which they had the fire, took off his iqal, and started hitting people right and left . . .

The commotion of yelling, screaming, and cursing became louder and louder, and the fire spread.

Abu Zahra yelled, "Fire, fire . . ."

All corners of the prison echoed, "Fire, fire!"

The prisoners ran out of their wards, panicking.

The Cat pulled his friend by the sleeve and said, "Hurry up, Imad, come!"

Imad thought that he was taking him away from trouble, but instead he led him towards the inside gate. The gate opened and through it came the five supervisors, panicking. They were supposed to be inside the prison at all times.

Imad and The Cat passed the inside gate towards the forbidden area between the two gates. The sky dropped a heap of hail like the beads of a rosary. At that moment, Sergeant Younis, carrying his baton, passed by them, crossing the space between the two gates without paying them any attention, and entered the prison.

The Cat whispered, "Run away, Comrade . . ."

They passed the exterior screen toward the main exterior gate. The Cat jumped, trying to pull down the little hinge, but was unable to reach it.

"Stretch your arm, Comrade."

Imad tried to reach it, but he could not. The noise in the prison courtyard became louder. The Cat urged him to try again and to hurry. "Quickly, we don't have time."

Imad stretched his hand again over the door frame and brought back a long crowbar, placed it in the lock of the exterior gate, ready to pry it open.

He raised his leg, looked at The Cat: "1, 2, 3 . . ."

They pushed on the crowbar with all their strength and desire to escape. The lock broke, making a loud cracking noise that coincided with the roar of the thunder.

The door opened.

(Oh, how wide is the sky!)

Lightning flashed as if it was making a crack in the wall of the horizon. He saw his mother's face blossom between the petals of jasmine flowers. She was not opening her arms; she was flapping her wings and calling, "Hurry up, Imad . . ."

He walked outside. The sky was dropping snowflakes that flew around like white feathers.

The guard, glued to his wooden hut, noticed them. He blew his whistle, got ready to shoot, and yelled, "In place. Stop!"

Saeed froze in place, panicking . . .

Firmly and with resoluteness, Imad threw the crowbar at the guard. It startled him, and Imad yelled, "Saeed, fly, cross the road."

Saeed ran down the few stairs at the entrance like a frightened cat . . .

Imad heard a loud screech, and suddenly saw Saeed fly.

He had been hit by Asaf's car, the small white Volkswagen. He saw Asaf swaying behind the wheel and watched the car hit the fence of Hanawi House.

The alarm bellowed through the prison.

A yodeling came from the women's prison.

The police rushed to the scene from all directions.

The sides of the hill echoed all of the sounds combined.

On the snow, Saeed lay, run over like a flattened poppy flower. His red blood spread out quickly and colored the snow, running down the hill to the city streets.

A handful of people gathered east of the Catholic church, covering themselves from the drifting snow.

A round of bullets from the guard's machine gun crashed between his shoulders . . .

He bent to the front, and then stood straight.

He felt the white feathers cover his head, shoulders, and stretch to his hips . . .

He spread his arms wide, exposed his body to the jasmine in the sky, filled his lungs with the wet air, tiptoed, saw Maha's face with all its freckles, fluttered his wings, and flew!

He flew high to where he could recognize the simplicity and depth of things.

The call to Maghrib prayer sounded.

NOTES

TRANSLATOR'S INTRODUCTION

1. *Banipal* 50 (2014). Selections of the novel also were reprinted in this issue.
2. The 27th night of the Month of Ramadan, the Muslims' month of fasting, also called the "Night of Power." Muslims believe that it is a holy night were all prayers are answers.
3. Hashem Gharaibeh, *Habat Ghameh* (A Grain of Wheat—Short Stories) (Amman, Jordan: Al-An Nashiroon, 2014), 77.
4. Ibid., 27.
5. The story appeared in his second collection of short stories, *Galb Al-Madinah* (Toppling the City) (Irbid, Jordan: Dar Al-Kandi, 1990).
6. This and most other references in the introduction are based on my translation of an unpublished interview with Hashem Gharaibeh on 6 April 2016.
7. Ibid.
8. See *You as of Today My Homeland: Stories of War, Self, and Love*, by Tayseer al-Sboul (East Lansing: Michigan State University Press, 2016) and his collection of poems, *Desert Sorrows* (East Lansing: Michigan State University Press, 2015).
9. Interview, 6 April 2016.
10. Gharaibeh in an interview with Amni Shukri for *Believers without Borders*.

11. Eiad Nassar, "The Cat Who Taught Me How to Fly, by Hashem Gharaibeh—A Narrative Museum of Life in Prison," *Akfar* magazine, no. 275 (December 2011), Ministry of Culture, Amman, Jordan.

12. A paper "Al-Ket al-lathy Alamany Al-Tayaran, min Manthur Gaston Bachelard (*The Cat Who Taught Me How to Fly* from the Perspective of Gaston Bachelard)," by Professor Ghassan Ismail Abdul-Haq, presented at the Jordanian Writers Society, Al-Zarqa, 15 March 2014.

13. The young Tunisian peddler who set himself on fire in protest of the harsh economic situation in his country and the attitude of indifference and disrespect that he received while trying to get a permit from the government offices to continue selling his vegetables. His action was the flame that ignited the wide-scale protests and eventually led to the revolution dubbed the Revolution of Cactus and Jasmine.

14. Interview with Amni Shukri for *Believers without Borders.*

15. See further details in the author's introduction.

16. Interview 6 April 2016.

17. This corresponds to the period Gharaibeh spent in this prison before being transferred to other prisons, where he spent a total of seven and a half years.

18. Tayseer al-Sboul is one of Jordan's most renowned writers and poets. His famous novella *You as of Today* documents the 1967 War from a Jordanian perspective. It was one of the first Arabic literary works about the '67 War, and won the prestigious al-Nahar Award for 1968. Michigan State University Press published the novella and his two short stories in translation (*You as of Today My Homeland: Stories of War, Self, and Love*, 2016) and also published his poetry collection in dual languages (Arabic-English) in 2015.

19. Hashem Restaurant is a famous, simple 24/7 restaurant that opened in 1959 in downtown Amman. A feature of the city, it is well known for being a gathering place for intellectuals, socialists, workers, tourists, and locals alike. The restaurant was visited during midnight in Ramadan in 2008 by King Abdullah of Jordan in recognition of its contribution to the city.

20. Tayseer committed suicide later that year. Read more about Tayseer al-Sboul's work and life in the introductions to *Desert Sorrows* and *You as of Today My Homeland: Stories of War, Self, and Love.*

21. He refers to the Zakaria Tammer novel *The Tigers on the Tenth Day.*

22. *Jonathan Livingston Seagull,* by Richard Bach, and *The Little Prince,* by Antoine de Saint-Exupéry.

DREAMS, MY NOVEL, AND ME: THE NOVEL *THE CAT WHO TAUGHT ME HOW TO FLY*

This was first published in *Banipal* 50 (2014). Translated by Nesreen Akhtarkhavari.

1. Hashem Gharaibeh was deeply influenced by Antoine de Saint-Exupéry's short story *The Little Prince* and Richard Bach's short story *Jonathan Livingston Seagull*. Both authors were pilots.
2. Members of the Bdool tribe lived in the caves in Petra until they were given houses in the mid-1980s with the land they had settled, an offer to them by the government in perpetuity as "Bedouin territory" in exchange for "liberating" Petra.
3. Al-Harith was a strong king who strengthened and expanded the Nabataean Kingdom and controlled the trade route in the region.
4. Baida (the white) is a semi-desert area close to Petra, designated "Bedouin territory" with permanent buildings prohibited.
5. The Bdool believe that the spring created by Moses to provide for his people was blocked by a dam built by the Nabataeans and channeled to carry drinking water to the city, creating the long "Siq," gorge, which is the main entrance into Petra.
6. Khalwat al-Bayadah (White Hermitage) is a prayer house and the primary sanctuary of the Druze.
7. *The Little Prince* was penned by writer, poet, and pioneer aviator Antoine de Saint-Exupéry (1900–1944). *Jonathan Livingston Seagull* is a fable by Richard Bach, first published as *Jonathan Livingston Seagull—A Story* (1970). During 1972 and 1973 it was a bestseller in the United States.
8. These are references to *The Little Prince*.

THE CAT WHO TAUGHT ME HOW TO FLY

1. This is a famous Indian song from old Indian films. Arab movie theaters used to play Bollywood films with subtitles.
2. *Shabeh* (suspension) and *Falagah* (flogging) are torture methods.
3. This is a political term that indicates giving up or betraying the Party.
4. Forty and seventy Falls are measurements of time used in various references in Islamic traditions.
5. A reference to the Sura: "A day of God is a thousand of what you count."
6. *Zaghruta*: A loud sound made by moving the tongue, performed at happy occasions and celebrations such as weddings and births.

7. Every ward is a sleeping unit, but every sleeping unit is not a ward. Each ward holds more than 50 prisoners.

8. Member of the Palestinian Liberation Front/Organization.

9. Loose, untreated tobacco.

10. A habit and belief that pretending to spit three times inside one's garment prevented the harm and bad luck that could be caused by an evil eye.

11. A standard statement used to publicly announce that the person gave up his party and pledged his loyalty to the government. This was perceived as "falling" (betraying the party) and resulted in being blacklisted by the party.

12. Haj, a title given to a person who completed Haj (pilgrimage to Mecca), implies piety and wisdom.

13. The Pasha was a title given to the highest-ranking military officer serving as the head of the Security Forces. The Pasha in the novel is the protagonist, Imad's, maternal uncle. The author of the novel's maternal uncle was also the Pasha when he was arrested and sentenced to ten years.

14. *Zogrut* is the common name of an insect between the bee and the wasp; its honey is not desirable and its sting is not feared.

15. An idiom indicating that living for a long time exposes the person to strange events.

16. *Alafsh*: Literally, "furniture." The common prisoners with no influence or authority.

17. *Alnawater*: The watchman, appointed to administer the affairs of the prisoners.

18. *Al-nuzala'*: The residents, the prison inmates.

19. *Al-asafer*: Literally, "sparrows." A title given to the prisoners who serve as informants to the prison administrators for small favors and perks.

20. *Al-tanabil*: Literally, "lazy ones." Refers to unsocial prisoners who go through their prison sentence without participating in any of the prison's activities or occupying their time with a hobby or a trade.

21. *Al foura* is the period during which the prisoners are allowed to get out of their quarters to the courtyard. The popular poet said: "Oh uncle, prison's guard, ignore what you see at the hour of *foura*."

22. A derogative reference to his skinny and small stature.

23. At the right of the entrance of the prison stood a screened visitors' area, a rectangular cage where the prisoners met their visitors.

24. The agricultural town where the author and his family are from and where he currently resides.

25. Turkish officers during Ottoman rule of the region were in charge of collecting taxes.
26. The prison was an old Ottoman government building.
27. "Tal" means "hill." It is also the name of a prominent family in Irbid province.
28. "Uncle" can indicate a family relationship, though not necessarily an actual uncle, or it can be used as a term of respect to an elder person.
29. Yarmouk University is in Irbid, where the author was attending school at the time of his arrest on political charges.
30. A prominent Communist Jordanian lawyer who defended many of the young political detainees when they were brought to trial, including the author. Many of the trials lacked due process.
31. Referring to the practice of placing a thumbprint in the bottom of an empty Turkish coffee cup after pouring out the thick residue in preparation for reading one's fortune by looking at images at the bottom of the cup.
32. The phrase translated as "just" here could also be translated to read "but."
33. *Gatayef* is a type of dessert made of a small pancake stuffed with nuts, cheese, or dates, baked and then soaked in syrup.
34. Some Arabs believe that too much laughter brings bad luck.
35. Mustapha Wahbi al-Tal, Jordan's first and most recognized poet.
36. One of the first chemicals in widespread use as a pesticide that later proved to be harmful.
37. In reference to a Quranic verse.
38. Ibn Tamim, a pre-Islamic poet who converted to Islam.
39. *Atawat*: The family of the aggressor is given time to gather the required monetary funds needed to appease the victim's family with the warranty of a third party that will facilitate the negotiation until an agreement is reached.
40. In reference to *Jonathan Livingston Seagull*.
41. In reference to Salah Abdul Sabour's poetic play *The Tragedy of Halaj*, which has a similar ending.
42. From a poem by al-Akhtal al-Sagher.